HONOR RESTORED

Guardians of the Fae Realms: Book 9
JL Madore

Honor Restored: Guardians of the Fae Realms

JL Madore -- 1st ed.

ISBN: 978-1-998372-66-9

FOREWORD

BEFORE YOU START!
Honor Restored is book one in Honor Thornebane's harem and
book 9 in The Guardians of the Fae Realms series.
If you missed the first two harems, and want the intro to how
we got here, you can grab the books below and start at book 1
of the entire series.
Guardians of the Phoenix.
Darkness Calls

If you don't want to, that's fine too. The story stands alone,
there might just be a lot of characters you don't know.
To that end:
Calli is the phoenix, and her guardians are Kotah (Wolf), Jaxx
(Jaguar), Hawk (Hawk...obvi), and Brant (Bear)

Keyla came next with Creed (Mind Guardian Fae), Dillan/Doc
(Bear) and Rhylan (Dragon)

Hope this helps.

Enjoy,
JL

CHAPTER ONE

Honor

I am Honor Thornebane, Princess of Dornte, Guardian of the Crown, younger sister to Creed. I am a strong mind guardian, and I will never give up my fight to free myself, my brother, and my quadrant.

The bitch queen who kidnapped me and locked me in the prison of my own mind will never break me.

I will never give up.

I take a beat and let my mantra sink in and do its work. A mind guardian locked in her mind isn't the worst thing that could've happened. I am strong. I will find a way to break free from this curse.

Lately, the dark loneliness of mental isolation has been lessened by the presence of a presence I've come to call my sexy shadow. He started visiting infrequently at first, now he keeps me company and soothes my soul.

A distant brush against my synapse.

A probe to my thoughts.

A question to be answered.

I try to call him when I can't bear the darkness but he comes and he goes on his terms. When he's with me, things don't seem so hopeless.

Part of me finds it alarming that I've welcomed him with such acceptance. He is inside me, after all. He's behind my walls. He knows me and sees things within me I would never show others.

I thought, at first, he might be an enemy trying to infiltrate. I don't think that anymore. Since his visits started, the magical ties binding me to oblivion have started to give a little.

Coincidence? I think not.

I believe my sexy shadow is doing it.

My dark knight.

My knight in the darkness.

By now, the magic he wields tingles over my skin with an oddly familiar flavor to it. It awakens my cells and reminds me I'm alive.

It's a delight I crave—a sensual treat.

When he's with me, I feel his erotic caress.

He cares for me. He may not be able to speak to me in words, but he speaks to me in other ways. It's in the strength he lends me. His persistence to fight the ties that bind me. The increased regularity of his visits.

And even though I no longer know if my body's been locked in Laryssa's lead vault for months or years, the presence of my sexy shadow breaks up the time and gives me hope.

I am Honor Thornebane, Princess of Dornte, Guardian of the Crown, younger sister to Creed. I am a strong mind guardian, and I will never give up my fight to free myself, my brother, and my quadrant.

Bring it on, bitch. I've got this.

My eyes snap open, and I squint at the brightness. My mind is a jumbled mess and my muscles ache, carrying the echo of fatigue and disuse. My limbs feel heavy, my blood crawling through my veins like it's clotted and thick. What happened? Where am I?

The light is piercing my skull.

I've been too long in the darkness. Too long in that stupid vault. I scan my surroundings and my heart lurches. I'm home...

My bed.

My belongings.

My private suite.

Shifting my legs beneath the covers, I'm relieved to find I'm wearing pajamas. With Laryssa and the brutes she employs to terrorize Dornte citizens, nothing can be taken for granted.

I battle with the fog dulling my wits and try to figure out how I got here. The last thing I remember is being ripped off the Traveler's bed in StoneHaven and shoved into that lead vault to rot.

Then nothing until the arrival of my sexy shadow.

I sigh and let my eyes fall closed. I'm tired and the memory of him is so soothing...

No!

I snap my eyes open and fight the pull to fall back under sleep's spell. *Fuck that.*

I've spent enough time sleeping and drifting around on the mental plane to last a lifetime—first when I projected myself into the Human Realm to ready Calli for her destiny as the phoenix. And then while I fought to not lose my sanity locked in that fucking lead vault.

To keep from drifting back into the druggy comfort of oblivion, I calm my mind and work to recapture the reins of my life.

I am Honor Thornebane, Princess of Dornte, Guardian of the Crown, younger sister to Creed. I am a strong mind guardian, and I will never give up my fight to free myself, my brother, and my quadrant.

I open my eyes again and assess the situation.

My bedroom is dimly lit, and I lay on the same bed I've had most of my adult life. Everything looks and feels the same, and yet nothing is the same.

My parents are dead. My brother is a puppet of the bitch queen. And I am her toy.

My body is whole but weak and sore. There doesn't seem to be anything holding me prisoner, but dollars to donuts there's an armed guard outside the heir's suite waiting for me to try to escape so he can strip me down and make me sorry for having a liberating thought.

The fog in my mind hangs heavy but piecing together the details is helping. Carefully, I ease back the covers and sit up. A rush of vertigo makes the room flicker dark as my hearing phases in and out.

Blood rush.

How long have I been lying here?

I wait until the violent threat of unconsciousness ebbs away and breathe deeply in and out.

As my bestie, Calli, would say—I've got this.

I swing my legs to the side of the bed, and they fall like weighted sacks of sand. There's a coffee mug on the floor and I knock it with the side of my heel. The poor thing careens across the carpet, spilling its contents, until it cracks into the bedside table.

Shit.

That crash is bound to bring the guards.

My time is limited. I'll never make it to the door in time to jump my captor, so I grab my legs, pull them back on the bed, and lay back down with my arm draped across my face.

Eyes opened a crack, I breathe deep to fill my lungs and make every effort to calm my racing heart.

Don't fuck this up, Honor, or you'll spend the next year back in that lead vault.

4

The door whooshes open with a soft hiss, and I ready myself for my escape. Instead of one of her mindless dragon thugs, it's a military man. He looks like a hot quarterback squeezed into a tight black polo shirt. Muscle-banded arms, trim waist...

"Honor, my name is Lukas. You are safe."

When he bends beside the bed to pick up the coffee mug staining my carpet, I swing with all my might and catch him across the back of his neck.

He goes down on one knee, but his reflexes are lightning-fast, and he spins, catching my bare ankle right before it connects with his side.

"I assure you," he says, his voice smooth and thick with an English accent. "Everything is fine. You are in no danger from me."

I've heard that before. "Calm down, Honor, they said. It doesn't have to be this way, Honor." I grapple his wrist and scissor my legs around him, pulling him onto the bed. Rolling onto my knees, I straddle his hips and pin him to the mattress. "It's the easy way or the hard way, Honor."

Something ignites in him and his pupils dilate. He's got the craziest gold flecks in the most beautiful hazel eyes I've ever seen. "I'm not putting up a fight here because you're not a prisoner. You're home."

"Who are you? What am I doing here?"

He opens his fists where I have his wrists pinned to the mattress and sigils appear on the fleshy parts of his palms. "I've been taking care of you on your brother's behalf. Creed reclaimed the throne and we rescued you. You are safe now."

"Why should I believe you?"

He chuckles. "I'm kind of hoping you don't. It's been a long time since a woman's gotten so aggressive with me in bed. I'm enjoying you asserting yourself."

As inappropriate as it is, my body weighs in on that. I don't know if it's me straddling his hips or the look in his eyes or the sexy accent when he speaks, but yeah, things are happening in the girly department.

I grunt and push off him, backing off the bed until my back bumps against the wall.

"The next round of treats are in the oven. This time I made us—"

I grip the arm of the man entering my bedroom and whip him onto the bed with the other one. The glasses he's carrying fly against the wall, smash, and leak down the mauve damask paper.

Damn, I am not being kind to my carpet today.

This man doesn't have the same chiseled features as the first. He has dark purple hair, deeply tanned skin, and the long, pointed ears of an elven race.

"Who are you?" I resume my place against the wall and take a quick glance into the living room of the suite I shared with Creed before the raids.

It's empty. "Creed! Are you here?"

When nothing comes back to me, I curse myself for falling for the lies.

"Your brother moved to the King's Tower a few days ago after his coronation," the military man says.

"Nice try. Creed would never leave me in the care of strangers to move into the royal residence."

"A lot has changed, Princess. Please, I can prove it." He holds up his wrist to show me a watch on steroids. It has so many buttons and dials I can't imagine how it works. "Calli is in the Auburn Suite across the hall. She's been sitting with you day and night."

I laugh. "And I walk out of this suite and straight into a platoon of guards. I don't think so."

"Then let me call her."

I point at him as he moves to touch the watch and launch. The guy with the purple hair rolls out of the way as I grab the military man's watch, unfasten it, and rip it from his wrist.

Scrambling back, I tilt, my legs unsteady. Gripping the edge of my desk, I steady my stance. "Did you think I'd simply let you call for backup?"

He chuckles again and the deep, timbre makes my pulse quicken. "You're safe, Honor. Honestly. You're getting yourself worked up about nothing."

The elf nods. "I am Shadow. I was brought to Dornte by your brother and his bride from the Human Realm. It's a time of healing for Dornte. The usurper queen and her witch have been destroyed. You are free."

It's too easy.

I wake up after two years of hell and all the bad guys are gone and my brother is king and married and has saved me? I steady myself and check my mind to ensure I haven't been breached. It would be exactly like Laryssa to fuck with the mind of a mind guardian.

Bitch.

"Creed wouldn't leave me here."

"He thought being in your old surroundings would help you find your way back."

"I need to get out of here."

"As you wish," the elf says. "You are not a prisoner. You need only to relax and hear the truth in our words. We are here solely to help you reconnect. Lukas has been using his abilities to remove the spell holding you under Laryssa's control. I am here to assist your transition back to the reality of this world."

My gaze falls on Mr. Tall, Dark, and Dangerous sprawled out on the bed. He's the one who's been removing the spell? He's my sexy shadow?

Lukas.

I swallow as my body responds to that. He couldn't be any better if I made him from a wish list.

I want to believe them. Can I believe them?

~

Lukas

I curse the moment Rhylan steps into the room unaware. Honor is pressed tight to the wall beside the door and despite being almost talked down, the moment he arrives she's in full-fight mode once more.

Rhylan pauses in the doorway, noticing Shadow and I on our backs on the bed, and I've almost got a warning out to let him know Honor is conscious and confused when she launches.

She yanks his right wrist and swings him around to face him, her fist soaring through the air and catching the side of his face. His head snaps around on his spine like he's a fucking owl and then her knee comes up hard and fast between his legs.

"Fucking dragon," she shouts.

"*Ohhhh*," Shadow and I hiss, both of us piking as our junk projects sympathy pangs of pain.

"Honor, stop." I roll off the bed and try to distract her while Rhylan coughs and pants through the assault. "So much has changed. Rhylan isn't with Laryssa, he's with Creed. He helped us reclaim the realm."

I'm talking to deaf ears... or rather her very fine ass.

She sprints out the door, and I grab my watch from the desk where she threw it. Tracking her through the living room of the heirs' suite, she makes a beeline for the door. Her long, silver hair brushes the rounds of her ass under a skimpy silk short set.

Damn, she's quick.

Especially for a woman who hasn't been on her feet for what —a month or more? But while she's quick, she's certainly not steady. Using the furniture to remain upright as she runs, she cracks her thigh off the entrance table before flinging open the door and launching into the hall.

Barreling out of the suite in a stumble, she collides straight into Brant.

"Where's the fire, sweetheart," he says. "It's good to see you up and—"

Another of her thrusting knee moves has the bear doubling over and grunting.

"Calli!" I shout, banging on the opposite wall as I race into the hall. "Calli, she's awake and losing her shit. Get out here."

I track Honor down the hall, pacing her, but not closing in. The last thing I want to do is spook her more by making her feel like I'm trying to cage or capture her.

As I jog up the hall, I tap my FCO watch and access the Phoenix Quint group. "Honor is awake. I need Creed or Calli at the suite now. A friendly face would go a long way here, people."

"I'm here," Calli says, running out of the Auburn suite, pulling a silk robe on over all of her nakedness. "Wait, Riley... or Honor. Yo, bitch, hold up."

That seems to get through Honor's panic, and she stops. Her bare feet squeak on the polished floor of the corridor and her hair swings around, hitting her ass as it falls still. "Calli?"

"Yeah," Calli says, pulling her blonde hair free from the collar of her robe. "It's me, but is it you? I mean, we were pretty sure we figured everything out, but—"

Honor does a one-eighty and runs back to hug her BFF. Calli is neither tall, nor built with a warrior's frame. Honor is both and towers over our phoenix girl.

"What the hell is this?" Honor says, touching Calli's belly. "You're pregnant?"

"Uh, yeah," Calli says, rolling her eyes. "That's what happens when you have four insatiable mates and no time to stop at the pharmacy because crazies are hunting you and trying to mow you down."

Honor chuckles. "So, it worked out then? You found your guardians and opened the gate? You got here? And then what?"

"You okay, Bear?" I pat the guy's shoulder. The shifter's grizzly other half means his shoulders are as big and strong as battering rams.

Brant clears his throat and straightens almost to his full height. "Yeah... although it's a good thing Calli's already preggers because my nuts may not come down for a year or two. I think the poor guys are lodged somewhere around here." He lifts his hand to his throat and swallows.

"What happened?" Calli jogs back up the hall. "Are you okay, sweetie?"

"I'll be fine. I don't think your bestie likes me much. Although, it generally takes more than one sentence to incite them to violence."

The look of horror on Honor's face is too cute. "I'm so sorry. I thought..." she looks at me. "You were telling me the truth? I'm free? Creed is king and Laryssa and the Blood Witch are both dead?"

"True story."

Rhylan steps out of the heirs' suite. The poor guy has one heck of a red splotch on his face from where Honor clocked him and he's not standing too straight either. He offers her a sad smile and leans on the door frame. "Creed is on his way. He and Keyla were in the city center meeting with displaced citizens, but they are coming straight back."

"Fucking dragon," Honor says, pressing back against the wall. "I don't care what I missed, I want you out of my suite and out of my sight."

Rhylan drops his chin and takes that hit too. "As you wish, Princess." He steps past her and stops, to look back. "For the record, I am truly sorry for my part in your suffering."

As Rhylan strides off, I feel for the guy. He's been shunned by pretty much everyone in his life but is finally building a family here.

Honor should be his sister-in-law.

I suppose that will take time.

Taking control of the drama, I point toward the open door to the suite. "Calli, why don't you take Honor back inside. Maybe between you and Shadow, the two of you can get a few pieces of the puzzle put back in place so she doesn't feel so disjointed."

Honor pushes off the wall and strides straight up to me. Stopping directly in front of me, she lifts her chin and meets me eye-to-eye.

Fuck me. There aren't many women who are tall enough to do that, and I admit, I find it sexy as hell.

"And who are you, again?"

"Lukas, the personal bodyguard of Calli's mate, Hawk Barron, head of security for the Fae Concealment Office, and member of the London Guild of Mages."

"Ah, that explains the accent. I should've clicked in to that and realized you weren't from this realm."

"Lukas is one of the good guys," Calli says, at her side. "One of the best guys. He's the one who unraveled the Blood Witch's curse. He's the reason you're back."

"You're a witch?"

"A mage."

Honor's gaze remains locked with mine and I match her aggression. After serving in Section 20 of British Military Intelligence, there is nothing about this that makes me uncomfortable.

I can take her posturing all night long. It's kind of sexy, actually. No, change that. It's extremely sexy.

"I don't like you."

"Maybe you didn't hear the part about me being the one who

pulled you out of that little mind trap you've been held prisoner within."

Something flares in her gaze but I'm not sure how to read it. "Oh, I heard, but witches and I don't have the best track record."

"Me either. Good thing I'm a mage."

Her brow arches. With pale skin and silver hair and eyebrows, her complexion is as fair as any woman I've ever seen... but those eyes. The two-toned purple of her irises is beautiful and locked on me like they are, they glitter with a challenge.

She is assessing my strengths as if she intends to best me. I catch her gaze flicking down to the gun holstered under my arm and my cock responds unbidden.

I find her as compelling in the physical world as I did while I worked with her mental energy.

She's more than a survivor.

She's fiery and tactical.

My earlier commitment to protect and care for her is over, replaced by intrigue and personal interest. It's been a long time since my restless spirit had the challenge of a worthy opponent.

But this is neither the time nor the place.

I lick my bottom lip and swallow. "Calli is waiting to head inside and catch up on girl talk, Princess."

Out of nowhere, my mind lights up with erotic images of the two of us sparring on a sandy beach.

We're hot and barely covered.

The sun is beating down on us, searing our skin as she throws me to the sand and straddles my groin. I could end the challenge without trouble, but why would I? I lay there as waves roll in, ebbing up my sides.

Okay, being this aroused in front of Brant is going to come back and bite me in the ass. The guy wouldn't know discrete if his life depended on it.

Forcing my urge to pin her against the wall and act out a few of the moves she's currently daydreaming about, I take the high road. "Your control will recover but it'll take time. Until then, be careful what you wish for, beautiful."

The fit of my black tactical pants is getting tight and uncomfortable… especially in the company of friends.

Her gaze narrows. "I'm sure I don't know what you're talking about."

I grin. "I'm sure you don't." Damn. it's been too long since a woman with this kind of passion looked at me like that.

"Stay away from me, asshole." She turns on her heel and storms back into the suite.

Oh, no. I don't think that's going to be possible.

CHAPTER TWO

Shadow

*W*ow. Is it hot in here or is it just the sexual heat burning off the two of them? From where I'm standing at the door to the heirs' suite, I'm graced with a front-row view of Honor and Lukas having a sexual stare-down.

As a therapist in the fae world, I've seen and dealt with some incredible attractions: soul-searings, fated mates, soul mates, blood singing, destined partners....

All of those things have one thing in common. You can feel the erotic potential at their first meeting.

If I didn't know better, I'd say Lukas and Honor were hot and heavy and about to rip each other's clothes off for a round of wild stranger sex.

But they just met.

At least in the physical world.

As a counselor, I advise against sex with people you don't know. As a man smelling the arousal of those two... I might approve. Oh, and I might like to watch.

As Honor pivots away from Lukas, she grabs Calli's wrist and drags her into the suite in her wake.

I meet Lukas's gaze. He isn't one bit fazed by the brush-off. If anything, things seem to have gotten much more interesting for him.

"Shadow?" Brant says, pointing at the open door. "Aren't you supposed to be joining the girls, my man?"

I dip my chin and follow the ladies, closing the door behind me. I don't want to disturb Calli and Honor in their reunion, so I head straight into the kitchen.

I was in the process of baking when I went into Honor's room earlier.

Sliding my hands into the oven mitts, I pull out the tray of cinnamon buns I made using Jaxx's mother's recipe. According to Keyla and Calli, these will heal all wounds and balm even the most battered souls.

I was practicing the recipe and planning on using Brant and Doc as my taste testers, but I suppose there's no need for a dress rehearsal now that the main event is in motion.

It takes little time to slide them off the aluminum pan and onto a cooling rack and while they cool, I power up my datapad and update Honor's file.

Day 12/ 4:35 pm/ Patient regained consciousness and despite an initial display of confusion and aggression, seems to be processing her changed situation with little difficulty. Emotions: heightened. Motor function: working but disjointed. Cognitive function: engaged at first contact but further assessment needed.

Note: The patient seems to have established an instant physical attraction to her caregiver. Watch for signs of this growing into a savior/victim relationship. After the trauma she's been through, the patient needs to assert herself without falling to others as a crutch.

After saving, I lock the file and slide the datapad into its case. With my work complete for the moment, I pull a plate free from the cupboard and fit as many of the cinnamon buns onto it as I can.

After stirring a spoon through the icing, I drop dollops onto the tops and watch the sugary layer melt.

With my offering ready, I return to the living room.

The royal residence is set up with two private bedroom suites—one Honor's and one Creed's—on the far ends of the space. They share a living room in the center and a kitchen to the right of the entrance. The living room is a vast area with two large couches facing each other with a long, stone table between them. There is a bar on the window wall and a door on the opposite wall.

Holding my offerings out, I announce myself as I come up the hall. "Ladies, a sweet treat to celebrate Honor's return to consciousness."

Honor scowls at me, but I don't take it personally.

"You don't know me, Princess, but I was brought to Dornte by a friend to help soothe some of the betrayals of the past two years and to help the citizens of Dornte move forward."

Calli's green eyes light up when she sees what I've brought. "Shadow, are these Maggie's cinnamon buns?"

"Her recipe, yes. Jaxx and I have been working on recreating them. I look forward to you telling me how close they come. In no way do I expect them to be as good as hers, but mayhap a close second."

"A close second will still be amazing," Calli says.

Honor is not as easy to please. "No offense, elf, but I don't know you and I'd like you to leave."

I'm about to reply when the door opens and Creed and Keyla rush inside. Both of them are dressed in their finery and Creed looks every bit the part of the king. "Thank the Powers, it's true. Honor, thank the gods. I can't even...."

I set the tray of baked goods down onto the coffee table and bow to the king and queen. "I shall leave you to your celebration, sire. Please let me know if you need anything of me."

"Thank you, Shadow," Keyla says.

I bow my head and leave them to their privacy.

Honor

When Creed comes into the suite, I'm bombarded with several waves of emotions in quick succession. The first wave, of course, is a rush of unfettered joy. I race forward and hug him, holding him tight. He's safe. I'm safe. And from what Calli was telling me a moment ago, the woman standing here is his wife.

I ease back and swallow at the lump pressing up at the base of my throat.

That's when I'm hit by the second wave of emotion.

Anger. Stepping back, I look at him and it hits me. He's fine. He's happy. No, he's not just happy, he's loving life while I've been suffering.

I was stuck in hell, fighting for my life and my sanity and he found the time to fall in love and get married?

"I have so much to tell you." He squeezes my hands and then pulls me back into his arms. "Oh, but first... this is Nakeyla. I'm not sure if Calli told you or how much she's told you yet, but once she opened the portal gate, the bitch queen took me through as her pet and the moment I laid eyes on this beautiful female, we were soul-seared."

I try my best to force a smile. Soul-seared. The universe left me locked in my mind and gave him a soulmate mirrored to him perfectly in every way. "Calli mentioned that. It's nice to meet you, Keyla."

I study the woman before me, and my mind shorts out. She's

a girl. A young, Native American girl who barely looks old enough to move into her dorm room as a freshman at college—and *she's* the queen of Dornte?

My mother was a queen.

She was regal and wise and deserved much better than to be slain and replaced, first by a maniacal bitch like Laryssa and then by this kid from another realm.

"It's lovely to meet you," Keyla says. "I'm so thankful you've come back to us. Creed has been sick with worry and now that you're awake, we can all work on healing the wounds—"

I hold up my finger. "Excuse me, but you don't get to talk like you understand what we went through."

"Honor." Creed's smile drains away. "Keyla is the reason we regained control of Dornte. She's the one who tracked you down in that vault and the one who made me strong enough to fight Laryssa and win. Don't discount her importance—"

"It's fine." Keyla presses a hand on his chest. "It's been a terrible time for you both and it must be overwhelming to wake up and be told what's been happening in the world without you."

I rub my fingers over my forehead. "You're right. It's overwhelming. I'd like you both to leave."

"What?" Creed looks horror-stricken. "Me? You want *me* to leave?"

"I do. My emotions are all over the place and I'm going to say or do something hurtful. I'd like to be alone with Calli for a while."

The devastation on Creed's face twists in my gut like a corkscrew but there's nothing to be done about it. I simply can't handle a reunion right now.

Creed pegs me with an eerie gaze and I can barely look at his ebony eyes without flinching. I have no doubt they are a residual of his curse. It's exactly something Laryssa and her witch bitch would do.

"I'll tell you one thing," he says. "I've imagined this finally being over for years and never once in my envisioning did you look at me like you're doing now. I'm sorry for whatever it is you blame me for, but don't send me away. I want to be with you."

I shake my head. "That's not what I want."

Keyla reaches forward and claims his hand. The two of them lock gazes and have a private conversation over their mental connection. I've seen my parents do that enough times to recognize it. Still, it upsets me that he would share that kind of intimacy with a stranger.

She's not even a faery.

After a moment, Creed frowns and turns back to me. "All right. I won't push. Take all the time you need."

He leads Keyla toward the door, and I fight the urge to call him back.

But I can't.

I don't know where all this rage is coming from but it's better that he leave with his child bride than for me to voice my opinion about him mating her and making her the queen of our quadrant.

When the door clicks shut, I exhale and sink onto the couch. "Can you believe that? Did you see that girl? What is she, twelve? I don't know what the universe was thinking when it put the two of them together, but give me a break."

Calli sits on the couch opposite me and for the first time since she burst into the hall, she stops smiling. "Keyla is turning twenty in a couple of weeks. She was born the Prime Princess in our realm, and the universe nailed it when she and Creed were matched up. She's smart, compassionate, and one hell of a political asset to your brother and Dornte. She's also my sister-in-law and I love her dearly."

Shit. "Sorry."

Calli waves away my apology. "This isn't about Keyla. There

was that moment with Lukas and Rhylan and now Creed. What is going on with you?"

~

Lukas

Six of us are loitering in the corridor outside the heirs' suite when Keyla and Creed come out only moments after they went in to see Honor. By the expressions on their faces, it is obvious the first meeting did not go well.

"What happened?" I ask.

Keyla lifts her chin and forces a smile. "She's overwhelmed and needs time to process."

"Wasn't four months in a lead vault long enough to be alone? Just asking." Brant holds up his massive hands and shrugs those muscled shoulders of his. "I expected her to be a bit happier to be home. Especially after everything you've all been through to get her here."

"We have the rest of our lives," Creed says.

Shadow pushes up from leaning against the door frame of Rhylan's old apartment across the hall. "Your sister has been through an extremely traumatic period in her life. Her parents were killed, she was violated more than once, and she has feared for her life and yours as well. Waking up and having all of that weighing on her and feeling the need to lash out and fight for survival is perfectly normal."

Creed sighs. "But those things happened to me too. How did I become her enemy?"

"Fash not, sire. You shall never be her enemy. Her actions and her comments are merely a reflection of her pain. She is in shock. Her body and mind have yet to process that her ordeal is truly at its end. It shall, indeed, take time."

Keyla seems to draw strength from the counselor's words

and pats her husband's hand. "Shadow's right. Let's give her time to realize she's safe and the fight is over. Calli's with her and will explain everything. She is safe and awake. The rest will come."

I nod. "It could be worse."

Brant lifts his shoulders and chuckles. "Knowing our luck, it could be much worse."

Shadow nods. "The thing to keep in mind is that with Honor awake, you are one step closer to putting the past two years behind you."

Creed exhales. "From your lips to the gods' ears, Shadow. I hope you're right."

"I am. You shall see."

Keyla reaches forward and squeezes Shadow's hand. "Thank you. Please keep us posted on how things progress. Honor made it clear she wants space right now, but when it's time to try again, let us know."

"You know I shall."

When the royal couple leaves, Hawk and Brant retreat into their suite, and Shadow heads into his. I consider returning to my room but figure I'll give the ladies a bit more time before interrupting.

"Lukas, would you mind joining me for a moment?" Shadow holds the handle of his door until I enter and then close us in. "Please, have a seat. There are a couple of points I wish to go over with you."

I follow him inside and wait while he opens the little icebox and pulls out two bottles. "Beer?"

I accept the bottle, pull out one of the wooden chairs, and spin it to straddle. "Why do I feel like I've been called into the principal's office?"

"I assure you, that is not the case." He opens his bottle and then passes me the opener. "I want to commend you on a job well done. I doubt anyone other than Calli and I truly understand the hours and commitment you applied to break the witch's hold on Princess Honor. It is no exaggeration to say her return to this world is because of you and your dedication to restoring her."

I take a long swallow of beer and let the icy flavor coat its way down my throat. "It's nice of you to say, but I'm not the pat on the back kind of guy. I did what needed to be done. End of story."

He rests his elbows on the table and leans forward. "I respect that. My second point is that sometimes in intense and intimate situations like the one you two shared, a bond can form. It can manifest as a need to protect or be protected, an attraction to one another, or a dependency that wouldn't have developed otherwise."

Uh-huh, here it comes. "What are you getting at?"

"That moment you shared with Honor earlier in the corridor. The one when you were locked in a stare. It was obvious the two of you were highly charged and sexually aware of one another. I simply wish to say it is not in her best interest for you to pursue a relationship at this time. There are a great many issues and emotions she needs to process and that will happen more quickly and efficiently if she's not dealing with emotional entanglements."

My watch beeps and I read the display screen.

When I look up, it is impossible to tell if Shadow is waiting for me to respond to that or what I'm supposed to say. I take another long drink, hoping for a quick buzz to hit and make this all fade away. "Is that all?"

He turns his bottle on the table and chases the dew on the bottle with his finger. "I suppose so. I thought it bore mentioning because the two of you share a suite and will be spending private time together."

That porn video she flashed into my head of the two of us

wrestling on the sand comes back to haunt me at exactly the wrong moment.

That's the kind of private time I'm hoping for.

I push to my feet, finish my beer, and set the empty on the table. "Not a problem. Hands-off and keep it in my pants. Got it."

CHAPTER THREE

Lukas

ell, that was a bullshit waste of my time. I stride out of Shadow's apartment and hang a left toward the public wing of Thornebane Castle. Why the elf felt he needed to weigh in on my personal life is beyond me.

I realize she's the princess of this quadrant and she just woke up after being a tortured prisoner. Hell, I understand what she's been through better than anyone.

I'm the one who went into hell to find her.

I'm the one who fought through the demented web of spells and wardings to cut her free.

I'm the one... aw, who are we kidding. The elf knows exactly what he's talking about.

I push through the double doors and storm forward, weaving through the highly polished halls. The faces of the castle staff are beginning to look familiar. For them as well it seems because they know enough to back up and get out of my way.

The stairwell that leads down to the lower level should have restricted access.

It doesn't.

I make a mental note to bring that up with Honor when she assumes control of crown security.

My boots thump out a thundering rhythm as I answer Rhylan's call.

Manifest an unhealthy dependency? What kind of bullshit psychobabble is that?

There is an obvious attraction—I started feeling it last week while I was probing her mind. She needed me. She took comfort in knowing she wasn't alone in her struggle to get back to the real world.

My soothing her and gaining her confidence was a kindness, not lechery. I'm not some horny college prat driven by conquest. I wasn't that guy even when I was a horny college kid.

I get to the bottom step and meet Creed coming down the corridor from another direction.

"Wow, you look like you're about to explode," he says. "Anything I need to know?"

I'm attracted to your sister and don't appreciate being cock-blocked by the elf counselor you hired to monitor her recovery. "Nope. S'all good."

He doesn't seem to buy that but doesn't push. "You got the call too, I take it?"

"Yeah, what's this about?"

"No idea. I was summoned by my mate, and here I am, coming when called."

I hesitate for half a beat to let him take the lead. Being pissy is no excuse for being disrespectful.

Creed is the king, after all.

Following the guy down the corridor, his long, silver hair flows behind those broad shoulders and black and turquoise wings. The contrast between silver and black is breathtaking.

He is a powerhouse and I'm glad I played a part in helping him regain his crown.

The guy is solid.

No airs of superiority or need to have people stroke his ego. He cares about his quadrant and its rule. He's tough, resilient, and smart. He will make a great king.

Honor has many of the same qualities.

It's too bad the first contact between Creed and Honor didn't go better. That's gotta hurt. He has busted his balls to get her home and supply the resources needed to restore her to the living plane.

And she gave him the cold shoulder.

That sucks.

When we get to the end of the hall, Creed presses his hand to the security screen and opens our way into the quadrant security center.

As we enter, Rhylan glances over from punching data into his tablet. The war table is up and running and I'm not going to lie, the military applications and intelligence protocols programmed into this baby give me an ops officer hard-on.

It's damned impressive.

The first time Hawk and I saw it, the two of us had so much tech envy we went to the manufacturer in Clarinta and put in our order to trick out the new Pennsylvania Prime Palace.

That's the beauty of your best friend and boss being a billionaire. Unrestricted access to all the cool toys.

"Thanks for coming," Rhylan says, waving us in. "You both know I've been monitoring the people who were actively supporting Laryssa during her two years of insanity. At first, I thought five primary supporters were working behind the scenes, but I don't think that's the case. If I'm right, there is one leader and the other four are following his lead."

I scan the holographic data sheets floating above the table

until they fall away and leave one profile up. "Ruic Breard. Well, he's not going to win any beauty contests is he?"

Creed curses. "And for a goblin, he'd be considered attractive."

"Glad I'm not a goblin then."

"Aren't we all."

"So do you know him?"

Creed nods. "Ruic is the head of a powerful clan of goblins and the CEO of Breard Industries, Dornte's ore supplier for our currency."

Shit. "You're telling me the man who controls the mint for your realm is the biggest opponent to your rule? That is not good."

"No. It's not," Creed says, taking a long look at the information Rhylan amassed. "I hoped with Laryssa gone, the corrupt members of the quadrant would return to whatever dark place they've been rotting in."

Rhylan shakes that off. "Unfortunately, if anything, there's been a surge of activity over the past few weeks. I programmed a bot to scan social media and private communication lines for activity by any of the five featured offenders. The patterns and trends surfacing are worth worrying over."

Creed frowns. "That's a huge violation of privacy, Rhy. It's not even legal."

The dragon shrugs looking unrepentant. "Technically, Laryssa's monitoring software was already in place and running. I simply haven't removed it from our system yet. It seemed to me that using it to catch the assholes who financed the past two years of hell was ironic justice."

Creed frowns.

I like it. "I'm with you, Dragon. Turn around is fair play. To catch scum, sometimes you gotta get a bit slimy. What did you find?"

Rhy reaches into the air before him and brings up an array

of photos. "The ones I marked with red tabs actively supported Laryssa and based on their comments and activities, are still a threat."

"And the ones tagged in orange?"

"Those are people Laryssa considered friends, but I haven't found any evidence they stand against Creed."

"Yet," I say.

"Yet," Rhylan agrees.

"Wow. You two are pessimistic," Creed says.

I shrug. "In a lifetime of working intelligence and security, I've learned it's wise to be a pessimist. Far fewer surprises come back to bite you in the ass."

Creed rakes his fingers through his hair and pulls it away from his face. The man is tall, broad-shouldered, and fair, like his sister, but those all-black orbs for eyes are more than a little unnerving.

A souvenir from the cursed form Laryssa and the Blood Witch inflicted upon him. Now that I'm done unlocking Honor's curse, I'll start working on Creed's.

"So, why are we here, exactly?" Creed asks.

He brings up the image of Ruic Breard again and hands me a datapad. "Two reasons. First, there have been increased mentions of 'Her' showing up all over the internet. The bots flagged the mentions and there are dozens of them, isolate Her, stop Her, take Her, remove Her as a threat."

I look at the two of them and frown. I don't want to cause a panic but—

"Do you think it's Keyla?" Creed asks.

Rhylan dips his chin. "I really don't want to think of her in danger but she is the sweetheart of the realm right now and she's swaying the views of a lot of citizens. They believe in her and her intentions to heal Dornte."

Creed looks ill. "You will ensure she's safe. I don't care how many men you need or what it costs. If these assholes are coming after my mate, I want them put down ASAP."

Rhylan nods. "There's no question about that. I'll work day and night to find them and end them. I swear."

"I'll mention it to the Quint as well. Hawk will want to help with the search and the security."

Creed nods. "I won't turn down help if it keeps her safer. If we had an Amberloq force, they would be the ones to handle it, but until Honor is stronger, I'm so very thankful that the two of you are handling things."

I nod. "You mentioned you called us for two reasons. What's the second?"

"This man," he taps the screen of the tablet and a picture of another man appears next to the goblin. "I've run his picture through every facial recognition agency we have in Dornte, the other three quadrants, and the archive database in StoneHaven. I have no idea who he is, but he's tied to whatever is happening."

I frown at the image of the blond male Hawk and I worked with for three years without knowing his true identity. "You can't find him in your systems because he's not from your realm, he's from ours. His name is Hunter Whitehouse. He's the former Director of Operations for the Fae Concealment Office. He's also Hawk's bastard half-brother and the only loose end we have in the plot to take down the FCO, Calli's destiny as a phoenix, and Kotah Northwood's reign as Fae Prime."

Rhylan takes another look and types in the information. "So, this is Sabastian's son. Laryssa was frantic to get in touch with him when she learned of Sabastian's death. Is he a hawk wildling too?"

"No. Hunter is a coyote—that's probably indicative of his duplicity. His mother was a domestic in their home some years after the death of Hawk's mother. Hawk didn't become aware of him until six months ago when he found out he'd been working in our office as a plant and the inside man in the plot to take down the FCO."

"Where was this picture taken?" Creed asks. "Is he here on our side of the portal gate?"

Rhylan nods. "It was taken two days ago in the downtown corridor. He passed by an empathic faery and she felt his dark and dangerous intentions. She had the owner of a storefront clip the image and send it to us as a possible threat."

Creed smiles. "That's wonderful. The citizens are banding together to keep the quadrant safe. Send her information to Keyla. I want to thank her and the store owner with a token of our thanks."

Rhylan nods. "What about Hunter? How worried do I need to be?"

I sigh. "It's hard to say. Hunter certainly isn't the evil mastermind his father was, so we might finally have the chance to take him into custody."

"But?"

"But he's been here two days, so if he's in Ruic's camp, they've likely already hooked up. He may not be the brightest Whitehouse, but he's got money and a stash of illegal weapons and that is more dangerous than the man himself."

Creed sighs. "Well then, we've got some catching up to do. Let's find him and see what he and his friends have planned for my quadrant."

CHAPTER FOUR

Honor

Calli and I lounge on opposite couches talking about old times and new and what I missed after my host body was killed by Sonny's men. Lying in bed for the past two weeks has left me drained and weak. I hate that feeling and promise myself that if I rest tonight, I will work out and start building my strength tomorrow.

But I'm not the only one running at half-power.

When Calli yawns for the tenth time, I take pity on her and sit up. "Baby making has seriously damaged your ability to stay up late and girl talk."

She chuckles. "Oh, the life I live. I have four sexy, insatiable mates, a cinnamon bun in the ole oven, and am the queen of a realm."

I hear the words coming out of her mouth and can't even believe she's joking about that. "The Calli I knew months ago would never have wanted any of that."

She swings her feet to the floor and sits up, setting her plate of sugary treats onto the table. "The Calli you knew months ago was forced off the road by a biker gang and died alone on the side of a country road in Texas. She went up in a ball of flame and was reborn to be more."

I draw a deep breath. "I'm sorry you had to go through that. When I learned they planned on bringing their illegal guns to this realm, I had to try to stop them. I never wanted you to get caught up in it, but thanks for taking him out. It was incredibly stupid… but sweet."

She rolls her eyes. "I couldn't let them get away with killing my bestie. I was a wreck. Seriously, I don't care if you're Riley or Honor. Don't ever die on me again."

"I'll try my best." The pain in her eyes spears me and I regret all the trauma she's gone through. "True to form, we toughed it out and are the last girls standing."

She holds up her fist to bump. "Hells yeah, we are. Nothing keeps us down."

True story.

I chuckle at all the funny sayings and idioms I got used to while living a decade with her. Time-splicing is tricky, but even though I wasn't really with her for ten years, I have the memories of those years and they are as real to me and dear to me as anything in the 'real world'.

"You don't know how hard it was not to lead you to your future," I say, tilting my head back and staring at the ceiling. "A million times, I wanted to tell you about our world and get you ready."

"Yeah, a heads up might've been nice."

"I know, but when dealing with the timeline and changing the outcome of things, if I had, I would've almost definitely ensured things *didn't* happen the way they were supposed to."

Calli shrugs. "Then I'm happy you didn't. Other than nearly killing Jaxx because I didn't realize I'm super strong as a phoenix, everything went sort of smoothly—sort of."

"I'm glad. I also want all the dirty deets about your four guys.

Is it you with them? Them with each other? A free-for-all of fornication?"

The blush pinking up her cheeks is too funny. "I'll spill but only if you tell me what the hell that moment with Lukas was about. The two of you looked like you were about to rip each other's clothes off and enjoy a wall-banger right there with all of us watching."

I force a laugh. "You're imagining things. You've got sex on the brain."

"I'm pregnant by four men. Of course, I've got sex on the brain, my hormones have gone wild."

I smile at my bestie here in my living room and with her four super sexy lovers across the hall. "You've come a long way from Jayson Burke's Superbowl party."

She looks at me and I can't tell if she honestly doesn't remember or if she's playing me.

"When he proposed his buddy, Nate, and you stay for an afterparty, you almost lost your mind."

The lightbulb goes off and her smile is so cute. "I was mortified they suggested I take them both into the bedroom. Two guys! Are you kidding me? No way."

I giggle. "Such a little prude. Who knew you were holding out for four?"

"Right? Two would've only been half as good."

The door opens and the dark wizard strides in like he owns the place.

"Excuse me." I shoot him down with a glare and rise to my feet. "I thought I told you to leave."

He closes the door and heads across the living room toward Creed's room. "You did and I did. Now I'm back. I'm working on a security threat to the quadrant. I need to change and get my vest. As you were, ladies."

So many things about that piss me off.

I look at Calli and whisper so only she can hear me. "What does he mean change? He's living here now?"

She grins. "He's been working night and day to break through the witch's curse and bring you back to us. When Creed moved into the King's suite with his mates, it only made sense that Lukas stay here."

"But I don't even know him."

"Now who's being a prude? *I* know him. He's saved my life a dozen times and Hawk's life a dozen more times than that. He's one of the best guys I know. If I didn't already have four men to keep me orgasming, I'd go for Lukas in a heartbeat... but if you repeat that, I will deny it and proceed to smother you in your sleep."

Lukas comes out at a half-jog, sliding a tactical vest over his head as he walks. "Don't wait up ladies. And don't worry, Princess, I'm housebroken. I won't make noise when I return. You won't even know I'm here."

He's about to get to the door and somehow, I'm standing in front of him.

He stops inches in front of me and my skin tingles with awareness. He's got the tall, dark, and dangerous thing going on and unlike most men, he meets my gaze without effort or any sign of backing down.

I'm not sure if it's his magic I sense or if the zing of electricity snapping between us is raw sexual chemistry.

That can't be natural.

Maybe all the time he spent connected to my mind has warped my ability to think straight. Maybe I just need to spend some time with him to prove to myself that my sexy shadow was a figment of my captive imagination. Maybe we need to bang like rabbits and get it out of our system.

Is it wrong to desire a night of sweaty orgasms to wipe away the frustration of what I've been through? No strings. Just me taking control of something I want.

My senses tingle, niggling at me to reach out with my gifts. What is he imagining when those hazel eyes grow hooded like that? What will he dream about tonight when he's naked in the sheets? What is wrong with me that I'm obsessed with asking stupid 'what if' questions?

"Did you need something, Princess?" His voice is deep and husky and when his gaze drops to my nipples poking out behind the silk of my camisole, a rush of moisture hits me between my legs.

I swallow, trying to steady my nerves before I speak. "What did you mean, a threat to the quadrant?"

"I mean bad men plotting bad things against your brother. Laryssa is dead, but there are other bastards who need to be brought to heel."

Standing as close as we are, I feel the heat of his body and sway toward him. "Calli says you're the one who killed her—Laryssa."

He makes no indication that he did or didn't.

"With your wizard magic?"

"No. With my gun. Two shots. One to the chest. One to the head."

Calli confirmed he was a military man. He looks like it. Hell, he feels like it. Being brought up with the Guardian of the Crown title hanging over me, I've always leaned toward the warrior types.

"Princess?" he says, looking anxious. "I'm here for you. Anything I can do, day or night, you need only ask. Do you need anything from me now? Can I answer any of your questions?"

Yes, please.

Why do my ovaries ache when you're this close? What did you do to me all those days and nights that got through the witch's spell? Did you mean to become my sexy shadow of seduction or was that a bi-product of us sharing that connection?

I can't ask any of that.

"It occurs to me you're stealing my job. You killed Laryssa. You're safeguarding the quadrant. Isn't that supposed to be the duty of the Guardian of the Crown?"

His expression softens. "Get some rest, Princess. There will still be bad guys for you to catch even if I help do your job for a while. Take a moment to regroup and gather your strength. In fact, tomorrow I'll take you down to the security office, and Rhylan and I will go over what we know and get you caught up."

Mention of the dragon traitor sends a cold shard through my guts. How could Creed love a man like that after what he did to us?

As much as I want to argue and go with Lukas right now to both assume my place at the helm of realm security and kick Rhylan and his brother out of my castle, Lukas is right.

I'm in no shape to get dressed let alone draw a weapon or go to battle. "Tomorrow then."

He nods. "I'll see you in the morning."

Lukas

Damn you, Shadow. I know she's recovering from a two-year ordeal and that she hasn't processed the PTSD and long-term effects of her time in captivity, but there's something about her that makes me want to wrap my arms around her.

Since when has that been my first impulse?

I'm not a hugger.

I close the door to the suite and meet Hawk coming out of the door across the hall. "Ready. You didn't mention Hunter to Calli, did you?"

I shake my head. "No. I figured it was better to let the two of them enjoy their evening. If I mentioned Hunter, she'd want to come with us to be there for you."

Hawk chuckles. "For a confirmed bachelor, you understand women really well."

I check the time on my watch. "And it's that understanding that allows me to slip the noose to remain a confirmed bachelor. See how that works?"

Hawk gives me a sidelong grin and it's obvious he's gleaned way too much from my scent. Stupid fucking wildling senses. "Yeah, I see how that works all right."

I grunt and shoulder-bump him as I storm past.

He chuckles and falls into step.

The two of us meet up with Rhylan at the back entrance of the castle. The dragon pulls up into the concierge area driving a black, muscle car, and waves for us to get in.

"Thank fuck," Hawk says. "I was beginning to think the only vehicles in this realm are minivans and shuttle buses. It's been a hit to my manhood."

I laugh, but he's not wrong. The conveyances, as they call them have been much too 'Driving Miss Daisy' for our tastes.

Rhy runs a caress across the dash and smiles. "I didn't get to drive my baby much with Laryssa running the show. Now, my life is my own again."

"I'll take the back seat," Hawk says, pulling a datapad out of the inside pocket of his blazer. "Lukas, you take shotgun."

I certainly won't argue that.

Sliding into the passenger's seat, I do up the harness and get settled. "Where are we looking first?"

Rhylan shrugs. "Using video surveillance and traffic cams, I tracked Hunter from the downtown corridor until he was picked up by a private shuttle rental. After a bit of hassle with the owner of the shuttle company, I found out your man was taken to a warehouse on the outskirts of the city. A preliminary search of the ownership on the warehouse didn't give us much, but when I dug deeper, I found that it's owned as part of Breard Industries."

"There's that name again," I say.

"Someone want to catch me up?" Hawk asks.

I give him the highlights about the leader of the rebellion being the goblin asshole who controls the production of currency for the quadrant.

"I can't see that ending well no matter what the outcome," Hawk says. "Why doesn't the crown control the currency? Allowing private interests to influence the economy of Dornte means it can be held for ransom."

Rhylan nods. "There were safeguards in place before Laryssa. Unfortunately, she waved the protocols in place making it much easier for Breard to seize control."

"So, where do we begin to fix this?"

Rhylan hits the indicator and takes us onto a ramp leading to the outskirts. "The fringe marshal in that area has done me favors in the past."

"Out of the goodness of his heart?" Hawk asks, looking up from his tablet.

Rhy shakes his head. "He is a coward and fears me and Vik. We may have played the part of Laryssa's evil enforcers a few times on him to condition his respect."

I chuckle and look sideways. "That's not respect, Dragon, that's intimidation."

He lifts a shoulder. "The old protocols supported using whatever means necessary to get the job done to the queen's standards. Laryssa might've been a horrible female and a selfish, crazy bitch, but she knew how to use fear and blackmail to keep people in line."

"Sounds like Section 20," I say, thinking about all the questionable things my team did for British Military Intelligence.

Hawk finishes whatever he's doing and grins. "I've ordered six SUVs and six Dodge Chargers to be driven through the expanded gate for us to use while we're here. Now that I know we don't have to be in mini-vans and sedans, we can ride in the style we're accustomed to."

"Thank fuck." I don't consider myself high-maintenance, but it's been hell not having a carpool.

Hawk nods. "Now, let's find my double-crossing coyote half-brother and reunite him with his wife in a joint prison cell."

"Conjugal incarceration. You're so thoughtful."

Shadow

It's nearly ten in the evening when I stride across the corridor to check on Honor. I am about to knock on the door to her suite when Calli exits, yawning and looking worn out.

She jumps when she sees me and then rubs a hand over the round of her belly. "Sorry. I think I was already half asleep there."

"You look it." I realize that might be taken in a less than flattering way. "You are resplendent as always, Prima... I only meant—"

She waves a weak hand in the air and sighs. "No apologies necessary. Are you going in?"

"If Honor will have me."

"She will have you," a feminine voice calls out from inside the suite. "Though I can't guarantee that I'll be good company. Calli has informed me that I am one cranky bitch."

Calli nods. "True story."

I reach to prop open the door and allow Calli to exit. "I shall take my chances, Princess. There is little you can say or do that will affect me."

"Then enter at your own risk." I wait until Calli's door closes across the hall before entering.

Honor comes out of Creed's side of the apartment with a packed bag in her hand.

"Where are you going? You woke up less than six hours ago. This is not the best time to jaunt off on a trip. Besides, you look like you need to lay down."

She casts me a quizzical look and then glances down at the bag in her hand. "Oh, no. This isn't for me. These things belong to the dark wizard who's staying here."

"Lukas."

She nods, her hair freshly washed and braided. "I was thinking about it while I bathed. I've never lived alone and now that Creed has moved on with his life, I think it's time I do."

I hear her words as well as the subtext behind them. "Isolating yourself is an understandable defense mechanism, though it may not be in your best interest."

"Why not?"

I move to sit on one of the couches and invite her to sit opposite me. "You were displaced for two years. It is completely understandable for you to feel unsettled and mayhap even like a stranger in your own life."

She frowns and sets the bag near the door. "What does that have to do with wanting the wizard out of my space? I don't know him. I don't trust him."

"Lukas is the man who brought you back to your life. He spent time with you while you were unconscious. Mayhap you find that intimacy unsettling after all you have been through."

She straightens and comes to sit across from me. "If that's counselor talk for not wanting a stranger staying in my apartment, then yes, you're right—I'm feeling unsettled. And the reason I was displaced in the first place was because of a person wielding magic. Him being a mage is unsettling."

I reach forward and rip a piece of cinnamon treat off a sugary coil. "Is it fair to judge him based on the fact that he was born to a magical family? You might look at things as if you are fortunate he is so skilled."

"I think you're presumptuous to think I've been thinking about him at all. Creed's child bride and Calli thought a wizard could counteract what the witch did. He did. That's over. Now he can move on with his life."

I chew my cinnamon triumph and tilt my head to the side. "I think your response is more about anger and feeling powerless in your own life. Mayhap lashing out and pushing away the people trying to help you is a coping strategy to keep you from getting hurt again."

She frowns. "Don't shrink me, Elf. I spent what felt like a decade in your realm preparing Calli for her quest. I worked through the things Laryssa and the Blood Witch did to me and my family. I'm good."

I lick my fingers and grab a napkin. "Then, if you're good, I shall leave you to your thoughts. If you change your mind, I am right across the hall."

"Don't feel bad when I don't come knocking. I appreciate that you're trying to help the citizens of Dornte, but the truth is, you're not one of us. You don't know what we've suffered and honestly, it's arrogant of you to think you can help us."

I stride to the front door and look down at the bag.

"At least I am here, and I am trying."

CHAPTER FIVE

Honor

*M*y sleep is restless, my dreams filled with images of disapproval and disappointment. Creed when I asked him to leave. Shadow when I asked him to leave. Calli when I mentioned Creed robbing the cradle and mating a child. Rhylan when I told him to get out of my sight.

Honestly, the only person who didn't seem to look at me with any kind of negativity was the wizard—mage. And even though I left his belongings as a hint that he's unwelcome, I feel his energy across the suite.

The guy can't take a hint.

Whatever.

Who is Lukas and why do I want to tackle him to the ground, spring his cock free, and mount him?

Did he do something to me?

Am I under his spell in some way?

In all honesty, I know it's nothing he's done intentionally. Still, I'm not accustomed to feeling this sexually needy. Sex for me has always been about mutual satisfaction and scratching an itch.

That's not what I'm feeling right now.

I can't quite put a name on it. My body-thrumming drive is tweaking my nipples and creaming my core. It's everything all at once and, at the same time, it's not nearly enough.

But what is it?

Desire?

Hunger?

Passion?

Whatever it is, it either needs to subside or get satisfied because me laying here scissoring my legs all night isn't doing me any good in the 'get some rest' category.

I close my eyes, but there's no use fighting it. There's no way I'll get any rest unless I take the edge off. Rolling off my bed, I pad barefooted across the plush carpet of my bedroom and press beside the hidden seam in the wall to open my closet.

When Calli and I went through here earlier, I was surprised nothing had been touched or taken. All my clothes have been sitting here awaiting my return.

It's like a shrine.

A memorial tribute of who I was two years ago.

At the back of the closet, I swipe the clothes out of the way and push on the pressure-closed panel. When I release my hold, it pops open, revealing my private safe.

It takes me the work of a minute to place my hand over the screen and tap in the numerical combination. When it opens, I swing the heavy door out of my way and smile. "Hello, boys. Did you miss me?"

Selecting the vibrator from the sanitizing station, I check the charge and smile. "It's like I never left, right?"

I forego the lube. First, I'm not sure what the expiration date is on that stuff, and second, with the rush of wet between my thighs, I don't need it.

Taking BOB, my Battery Operated Boyfriend, back to bed, I prop up my pillows and settle in. Then, I think about Lukas across the suite, jump up, and double-check the lock on my door.

Definitely locked. How embarrassing would that be?

I can just picture it... *I'm sorry, Princess, I heard you groan and thought something was wrong. I thought you might need my sexy warrior skills to soothe you.*

I shake my head. Lukas is not welcome in this endeavor of mine. Who needs a man? BOB and I are self-sufficient. If I wanted Lukas involved, I could go across the hall and seduce him.

I've seen the wanton in his eyes. He's as hungry and caught up in this post-spell madness as I am.

He should've been more careful when he was messing around in my head.

Lying back on the mattress, I hook the waistband of my pajama shorts and pull them off. It wouldn't take much to seduce him. For a guy in the intelligence industry, he's certainly not that hard to read.

He wants me. Maybe it's a hero complex thing or maybe he is feeling the effects of being overly intimate with me too.

Doesn't matter. That's the beauty of vibrators.

No strings orgasms and you don't have to make small talk afterward.

After a deep breath in and then a long exhale out, I drop my knees open and reach between my legs.

Yeah, this won't take long.

I may have been sexually active and even a little promiscuous in my host body, but this body hasn't felt the love for two long years.

"Okay, BOB. It's you and me, my old friend. Let's get our sexy on."

With my fingertip gently circling my clit, I reach down with my other hand and slick the dildo in my folds. I close my eyes and let the velvety silk of the cock's exterior caress away all the cobwebs of disuse.

Yeah. I remember how this goes.

Wriggling my hips, I slide my butt down a bit and get a better angle to—Oh yes, much better.

BOB is deliciously thick and long with the most amazing extension that reaches up and perfectly tops my clit. After lubing him up and a few gentle ins and outs, I turn on the vibrator.

My breath escapes in a rush and I'm lost to the bliss of stimulation.

That's what I'm talking about.

So good.

Dropping my head back, I ride the wave and take it all in. My life might be a mess, but this is simple and straightforward and well within my control.

Cock in and out. Vibrator on. Clit getting the attention it's craving...

All is right in the world.

I swallow as the tightening of my inner muscles starts to build. It feels so good. I dig my heels into the sheets and open my legs wider. It's too good. I don't want it to end yet.

You're safe, here. Whatever you need. The husky English accent of my sexy shadow invades my mind and I push it away.

Lukas isn't welcome here.

This entire self-pleasuring session is to take him off the table of desire.

It's been a long time since a woman's gotten so aggressive with me in bed. I'm enjoying you asserting yourself.

My mind flips back to that moment... me straddling him right here... on this bed... my legs split over his hips and me hovering over his—

The tension of my release grips inside and the pulsing clench and release pulls me toward my climax.

No. Not yet.

Dammit, he's got the most beautiful hazel eyes I've ever seen. And the way he stares me down...

I'm not putting up a fight here.

The keening of sensation is building. It's a wall of promise rising above me. My nipples ache to be sucked. I want his tongue to swirl and taste my skin.

Princess, I'm here for you. Anything I can do, day or night, you need only ask.

My mind guardian gift makes it so memories are remembered with perfect clarity: the heat in his gaze, the faded scent of his aftershave late in the day, the uncertainty in his voice when he said he needed to leave.

The thought of him leaving steals my breath. He can't leave... at least not before he and I work through this sexual obsession I'm suffering from.

Giving up on pushing him out of my mind, I embrace whatever it is that's pulling me toward him.

It's fine to fantasize alone and in bed like this.

Now instead of memories, I imagine Lukas pressing me into the mattress and pushing his cock inside of me. With a stronger hand, I pump the vibrator rubbing the nerve endings inside me and hitting my clit with each thrust.

It's been a long time since a woman's gotten so aggressive with me in bed.

I want that. My arm is starting to ache, but I'm not finished. I need more of him. His weight pushing down on me. His breath warming the side of my neck.

Yes. I want that. I want him...

And then, he's there...

One second, I'm fucking myself with the vibrator, thinking of him, and then I'm connected to him on the mental plane. He's naked in his bed across the suite gripping his cock and tossing himself off.

Gawd he's so hard and horny.

His breath saws in and out of his lungs, his free hand sweeping across those chiseled abs and up to his pec.

He grunts, breath rushing from his throat as his muscles clench, and he spills streams of cream over his hand and across that sexy pelvic 'V'.

I pull BOB in hard as my world shatters.

Sensations bombard, his and mine, and I'm lost to the throbbing bliss. I squeeze my legs together, riding out the ebbing waves of pleasure with that vibration trapped right where I need it.

The orgasm is delicious and I hate that it ends.

When my breathing slows and my knees fall open, I pull the vibrator free and turn him off. "You did good, buddy. Just like old times."

Only it wasn't like old times. I've never connected with an object of my desire without meaning to before.

Are my powers wonky after coming back online or has the magic of Lukas's efforts formed some kind of a link between us?

Either way, that shared orgasm is going to make breakfast awkward in the morning.

Yeah-no, I'm not ready to deal with that.

It never happened. What orgasm? I don't know what you're talking about.

Yeah. That's my story and I'm sticking to it.

Lukas

It's mid-morning when I finally drag my ass out of bed and surface for the day. After having my shower and getting dressed,

I leave my room and head straight for the kitchen to get a cup of coffee. I never used to be so dependent on a caffeine jump start to my day.

I blame Hawk for the weakness.

That man is a coffee whore.

When I round the corner and enter the kitchen, I'm surprised to find a pot of coffee waiting. Over the past week and a half, I've gotten used to a routine.

Shower. Brew a pot of coffee. Read the security updates on the datapad Rhylan hooked me up with.

But that was before Honor woke.

Something tells me nothing will be routine now.

"Help yourself to java." Honor is sitting at the small table in the corner, sipping at the edge of her mug. She doesn't look over to greet me. She doesn't offer me anything beyond the invitation to share the coffee.

It's not a warm welcome but it's a gesture.

"Thanks. Don't mind if I do."

I pour myself a cup and grab one of Shadow's latest baking experiments. After finding the cream in the fridge, I'm all set. "I hope I didn't wake you when I came in last night. It took me a bit to find my stuff and get settled. It's the craziest thing, all my belongings were packed and by the door."

"Yeah. That might've been a kneejerk reaction to sharing my space with a stranger."

"Any stranger or me?"

She meets my gaze but gives me nothing. "What's the difference? I met you yesterday. I don't know you. That's the very definition of a stranger."

I stir in the cream and *tink* the spoon on the side of my mug. After taking a tentative sip, I swallow and meet her gaze. "You know me, Honor. You may not want to admit it, but you do."

"Don't. I've already got one brother-appointed shrink telling me what motivates me. I can't take another."

"Fair enough. I'll leave the comments about your motivations to the professional. How did you sleep?

She swallows and sets her mug on the table. "Like a baby. Laid my head down after Calli left and didn't bat an eye until half an hour ago."

I chuckle. "Really? Did nothing stir you? Nothing aroused you in your slumber?"

She arches a brow and frowns. "I think the term you're looking for is *roused* me from slumber and the answer is no."

I grin, leaning back in my chair. "Uh-huh, did Calli mention that as well as tactical insurgence and military logistics, I'm an expert in interrogation and body language. I'm basically a human lie detector?"

She glares up at me and I can't help but smile.

"And even if I weren't, one thing I love about fair-skinned people is that their embarrassment flushes beet red. It's quite a visceral tell." I hold my finger out and point toward her cheek.

She slaps my hand away and reclaims her mug. "I don't know what you're getting at."

"No? I got in around three a.m. and once I got settled, I could've sworn we shared a moment."

"At three in the morning? No. Maybe you were drunk. Are you sure the threat to the quadrant really kept you occupied until three a.m.? Maybe you went out drinking and whoring afterward."

I choke on the dark roast and grab a napkin from the center of the table. "Sorry, no. I don't do a lot of drinking and whoring. That's not my scene. *Annnd* I was with the husbands of your brother and your best friend."

She takes another sip as if giving herself time to think of a change of subject. "So, what was the threat?"

I spend the next ten minutes explaining to her about Hawk's dysfunctional family and how we took down his father, but Raven and Hunter got away. "Rhylan helped us get the goods on

Raven a few weeks ago and we arrested her. Now we need to find Hunter and end this."

"And he's here?"

"He is. The bigger question is how. The portal gate to the Human Realm hasn't opened to the public yet so there haven't been travelers back and forth. Yet, somehow, Hunter made it here."

"What are the possibilities?"

"Either he bribed someone in our camp to let him pass through—which I highly doubt—or now that the seal between realms is broken, he found another gate to come through. Hawk's father was ahead of us on opening the portal gate, we just happened to have the key."

"Calli?"

"Yeah. She and the quint combined their powers to create the rift. It was the one part of the process Sabastian Whitehouse couldn't buy or steal."

"And that's how you think he did it? By creating a second gate somewhere?"

I cut my cinnamon bun with the side of my fork and shovel a large chunk into my mouth. "I do."

"And that means your bad egg has ungoverned access to my quadrant."

"For the moment, that's what we're thinking."

"Creed must be pissed."

"He's concerned more than pissed. There's no use in being angry. We simply need to shut it down."

"And how do we do that?"

She seems genuinely interested and less hostile about it, so I pull the information up on the datapad and set it on the table for her to look at. "Rhylan has the network of corruption nailed down to the leader and his followers. The man at the top of the dung heap is Ruic Breard, a goblin big shot."

She makes a face. "He's a major creep. Goblins aren't the

most endearing people, to begin with, but Ruic is an exceptionally horrid man. Greedy. Cruel. And as immoral as they come."

"Well, we're onto him now and closing in on the workings of his organization. With any luck, we'll shut him down before he has a chance to do any damage to the Dornte economy."

"Good. Dornte citizens have been through enough."

"Agreed. Rhylan has a few things he's checking this morning and then we'll be back at it. We'll figure it out."

Running a finger around the rim of her coffee cup, she shakes her head. "I don't understand how Creed can stand to be anywhere near that man. He held us prisoner. When I escaped, he dragged me back to Laryssa and I know it was no different for Creed."

"He also sympathized with Creed and watched out for him despite it costing him his place in his brood, with Laryssa, and almost his life. He risked everything to get on the right side of things."

"Too little, too late, in my opinion," she huffs.

"And you're entitled to your opinion, but Creed chose to forgive him. The guy was sold into servitude by his alpha and if he stepped out of line, his mother paid the price. It's not that different from what Creed was forced to do to keep you and your mother safe."

"Our mother died the night of the raid."

"He didn't know that. He only found that out a couple of weeks ago. All this time, Laryssa used the threat of her captivity as well as yours to keep him in line."

That seems to shake the foundation of her anger, but she shuts down almost as quickly. "I don't know why we're talking about this. It's none of your business."

I take another sip of my coffee and swallow. "Maybe. Or maybe since your best friend and my best friend are now mates, it means we'll be in each other's lives going forward. I respect the hell out of your brother and what he's trying to do here, and

I know Kotah, Calli and the quint are committed to ensuring all of that goes smoothly for Keyla and Doc."

"So, everyone is one big happy family, is that it?"

"Something like that."

"Then why do I want to throat punch everyone and rip their heads off?"

That's the most honest she's been all morning.

"Because you are stuck in a state of fighting for your life. You didn't get to work off your anger. Every survival instinct you have is still firing for you to make them pay... only they're both dead and so you have nowhere to put that."

"I thought you weren't going to shrink me."

"It's not me being a shrink. It's me being ex-military and nearly going off the rails because I didn't know how to adapt to society with my specialized and somewhat lethal skill set."

"Lethal? Should I be worried?"

"Not unless you're planning to kill someone I care about or overthrow your brother."

"Not on my agenda, no."

"Good, then let's address your anger and diffuse it before it becomes a problem."

"Don't worry. It will pass."

"Likely not before you do something you regret." I hold out my hand and smile. "Come on. Trust me. I know the perfect way to level you out."

She looks at my extended hand and laughs. "What have you got in mind?"

"Part of your recovery is physiotherapy and rebuilding your strength. If you want to throat-punch someone, I offer myself as tribute... if you can land a punch that is."

She grins and it's the first unguarded moment she's ever offered me. "All right, give me a minute to change and I'll meet you in the living room.

I set down my half-empty coffee cup. "You're on."

CHAPTER SIX

Shadow

Sitting in the great room of the King's Tower, I finish discussing the preparations for the memorial celebration. Keyla, Creed, Rhylan, and Dillan are going over the details and I'm waiting to hear their final thoughts. There should not be anything unexpected. We have discussed things enough that I think we're on the same page.

And yet…

"Is there something wrong, majesty? Have I missed something?"

King Creed passes the datapad. "No. I'm sorry, Shadow. Everything is exactly as we planned. I'm sure it'll be a lovely event, and you're right, having a memorial in the city center gives us all a place to grieve our lost ones and celebrate new beginnings."

Keyla takes my hand. "I've spoken with some friends and the response is overwhelmingly positive. I think it'll be a fantastic event."

I do as well.

Creed smiles, but I see how worry weighs on him.

"Sire, is there something more than your sister, weighing on you?"

He looks at Keyla and takes her hand. "There's reason to believe the rebels might be targeting Keyla. I've tried to convince her to stay home, but she won't."

"No, I won't," Keyla says. "I will be standing at your side when you address the citizens and they will see how committed we are to a new beginning."

Creed looks at me and sighs. "I'm surrounded by stubborn women."

I chuckle. "If I may, sire, Honor woke less than twenty-four hours ago. She will come around."

Creed nods. "I believe that, but she and I were always so close. Why can't she look at me? I've done nothing but worry myself sick over her for two years and she can't be in the same room as me."

I try to find the words that will ease him. "Honor has suffered through a lot—you both have. It is a tragic situation and there are many complicated and overlapping emotions. With siblings, feelings are deep and can be painful. Her keeping you at a distance is likely her way of keeping things simple while she processes."

Keyla squeezes my arm. "You'll keep working with her, won't you?"

"Of course, Princess."

Creed nods. "Will you mention the memorial to her? I would like her at my side when I unveil the statue of our parents... if she's up for it."

"I will, of course, mention it and encourage her to think about it." I know he's not getting the reassuring answers he's looking for, but healing isn't an instant thing. "Might I make a suggestion, sire?"

Creed chuckles. "Always, Shadow. You don't need to be so formal with me."

I disagree but that is neither here nor there.

"In the next days or weeks, might there be a tradition you shared with your parents that could be revived to make Honor feel more included in your new life? She lost her parents, as you did, and it might help if the two of you reclaim something of them."

Creed sighs. "What are you thinking?"

"Did you have a family ritual you shared or a special dinner or something that was only for the four of you?"

"Yes, I suppose there were quite a few things we did like that, dinners, star-gazing nights, fireworks, playing candlepins."

"Good. Then mayhap you could think of a way to include Honor in the restoration of one of those. At first, make it solely about you and her. Then progress to include Keyla and your other mates."

Keyla reaches up and slides a gentle finger across the king's pinched brow. "That's a wonderful idea, Shadow. We'll give it some thought and figure out the perfect way to set them back on track. Thank you for your help."

"Save your gratitude for when things improve... and they will. With patience and understanding, Honor will be her old self before you know it. We simply need to treat her with kid gloves."

Honor

The slap of Lukas's foot to the side of my face knocks my head spinning on a swivel and I hold up my finger for a second while the world spins. "Damn. You don't believe in pulling punches for a lady, do you?"

Lukas barks a laugh and points to his split lip. "Not when I'll be eating with a straw for the next two days."

I straighten and check my stance. When the world is level and steady, I check the wraps on my knuckles and make sure they are tucked and tight. "Heir's suite audio, play music, Whitesnake."

As the hard rock guitar riffs of Still of the Night sound off, Lukas's head starts to bob. "I'm impressed. I didn't know your realm celebrated hard rock."

I shake out my shoulders, the music fueling my energy. It's been a long time since I worked out but yeah, now that it's happening, I'm loving it. "Through the Travelers program, this realm adopted many of the Human Realm customs and habits. But honestly, Whitesnake is from my time living with Calli."

I step back into the center of the living room to go again. The couches are pulled back to the walls and the stone table has been moved.

It leaves us plenty of space to spar.

A zing of adrenaline fires in my cells and I stretch my neck out from side to side.

"You ready to go again, Princess?"

"Definitely. Let's see what you've got, wizard."

"Mage," he corrects.

I can tell that it bugs him when I say that, and I decide to let that go. He's obviously not cut from the same cloth as the Blood Witch, so it's not nice to paint him with the same brush. "Right. Mage it is then."

He dips his chin and I pat myself on the back. "Come and get it, Mr. Mage."

The sound of his amusement is lost in the rocking music, but I see his chest bounce as he laughs. He stripped off his shirt and socks and wearing only black workout pants and a cocky smile, I have to admit, I'm not hating the view.

He comes at me, feigns a strike, and when I don't fall for it, he winks. "Let me know when you're getting tired. You've been out cold and flat on your back for a long time. You'll have to build up your strength."

While he's chatting, I move inside, switch legs, and throw a kick up to his hip.

Lukas catches my ankle, spins me around, and drops me to the floor. Two hundred and fifty pounds of muscled male pinning me down could set me off after past assaults. It doesn't.

For some crazy, stupid reason, I *do* trust him.

He rolls off me the moment he tags his point and reaches out a hand to help me up.

"FYI, Shadow warned me off you but I gotta admit, I'm getting some hot and heavy vibes, Princess. If I'm imagining it, tell me now and I'll step back."

I slap my hand into his and let him heave me back to my feet. "You don't mince words, do you?"

"Who has time for that? One minute I'm in the Human Realm tracking kidnapped kids, the next I'm running logistics for Calli and Hawk in their crazy quest to open the portal, the next I'm in the Fae Realm hunting witches. Life is busy. Why waste time?"

The two of us step in close and start kickboxing. I've got my arms up and am blocking him well enough to keep from getting my ears boxed, but I doubt I'd win a fight of hand-to-hand against him if he was giving it his all. At least not yet.

My arms are aching, and my legs feel like they're getting rubbery. I know I should call it and stop, but I don't want to give this up.

I feel powerful with him like this.

I try for a right hook but I'm late and he ducks to the side and grabs my arm without effort. Pulling me tight to his chest, he holds me close and stares into my eyes.

"You're tired, Princess, and you're getting sloppy."

He's got my arms pinned and I wait for him to let me go. It doesn't happen.

Sweat is glistening on his forehead, but other than that, he shows no sign of a workout. Unlike me. I'm drenched and panting and ready to drop to the carpet.

"Why did Shadow warn you off me?"

"Something about me developing a savior complex and you becoming too dependent when you need to stand on your own."

"I think I'm standing just fine."

He offers me a sexy grin and drops his gaze to my heaving bosom. "I agree."

The click of the door unlatching has Lukas stepping back and releasing me. The sudden freedom is almost too much for my muscles to support and I bend over, bracing my hands on my knees.

Calli's mate—the bear—comes inside. I call out to stop the music, take a deep breath, and fall on my sword. "Brant, right?"

The guy is a hulk of a man with a playful smile and curly brown hair that hangs past his shoulders. "That's me. Calli explained everything to you about us being mates, right? You're not going to nut-bust me again?"

I wince. "No. And I am so sorry I did. I was panicked and thought… well, you know what I thought. I was wrong. I apologize for the cheap shot."

To my surprise, he cracks a smile and waves my apology away. "You're not the first female to nail me for no good reason."

"Let's hope I'm the last."

He chuckles. "Yeah, let's hope."

Lukas steps around me and lifts his wrapped knuckles for a bump. "Brant is an enforcer with our policing agency and one helluva fighter. I'm not sure what you and Calli covered last night, but when the chips are down, we've got quite a deadly team."

She said as much. "There's still a lot to catch up on, but we hit the highlights. She mentioned your other two mates are joining us tonight?"

Brant nods. "Yeah, Kotah had some Prime business to take care of back in the other realm, so Jaxx went with him to check on the progress of our new house being built on the portal gate property. They'll be back tonight. Calli didn't want to be away from you, and we can't stand to be away from her."

"It's nice that it all worked out for you."

The grin on his face is nothing short of radiant. "Yeah. The five of us lucked out. The universe knows what it's doing, that's for sure. Same thing goes for Keyla and your brother. They're great together."

I don't know what to say about that. How can my brother's mirrored soul be a nineteen-year-old princess from the Human Realm? I know the legends of soul-searing but don't get it.

Lukas seems to sense my discomfort and claps his hands together. "All right. That was a good first session. How about we both get cleaned up and then I'll escort you down to the security office. I promised you a rundown of the security issues."

Honestly, I'd rather have a hot bath and flop into my bed, but I don't think that's an option. As Guardian of the Crown, it's my duty to handle quadrant security as it was my aunt's duty before me.

Valorous failed.

I won't.

Lukas

When the water turns on in Honor's suite, Brant helps me move the furniture back into place. Once that's done, I take him into the kitchen. There's no question that's why he's here. He heard there are cinnamon buns and he's craving some of Maggie's magic.

"So, how's she doing?" he asks, tilting his head toward Honor's suite.

"Better. She's a bit shaken up and not a hundred percent physically, but it's only been one day. Why do you ask?"

"Calli worries and we worry when Calli worries. Stress isn't good for the baby, you know."

I know. Everything in their world right now revolves around that baby. I've never seen four grown men change the direction of their life so fast and so thoroughly as they have.

"Hey, can you do me a favor, Bear?"

"Yeah, of course."

I jog into my room and grab a USB key from my desk. "When you go to the portal hub to pick up Jaxx and Kotah, can you take a facial recognition file to the security office and have them upload it?"

He takes the drive and slides it into the pocket of his jeans. "And who are we putting into the system?"

"Hunter and his known associates from our realm. I figure if he's here, he might bring his crew for whatever he's got planned. It'll likely amount to nothing but we need to cover all the bases."

"Do you really think Hunter is sitting on a secondary portal gate?"

"I do. And if he is, that's bad news. From what we know about the Sovereign Sons and their illegal gun and drug running up the Pacific Coast, there are a lot of weapons unaccounted for. If Hunter is importing weapons from our realm into this one, that's on us."

"Yeah. We gotta clean up our own trash."

After checking my watch, I hand him a covered plate with five cinnamon buns on it. "I need to change before I take Honor to the security office to catch up on the state of the realm. If you see Hawk before me, let him know the trucks have been shipped and Rhylan is sending drivers to pick them up."

"Trucks? You mean manly vehicles that I won't have to slouch in?"

"That's what I mean."

"Yeah baby," he says, grinning from ear to ear. "Cinnamon buns *and* trucks. Today is a good day."

"Yes, it is. Let's hope it stays that way."

CHAPTER SEVEN

Honor

How many times did my father drag me down into the bowels of the castle to show me how the security of our quadrant worked? In truth, it wasn't his job. He was the king. In Dornte, that made him the Guardian of the Quadrant. His sister Valorous was the Guardian of the Crown. She was my predecessor and if life was as it should be, she should've been my mentor.

Valorous should've been a lot of things.

She should've lived at Amberloq Hall and watched over things in the castle instead of living off on her own.

She should've trained me and readied me to assume my role as the leader of the Amberloq.

She should've been part of our family and cared enough about us to overlook a few arguments with my father to serve the people.

I don't know all of what she and my father fought about when we were kids, but their failure to put it behind them and work together for the good of the realm cost hundreds of people their lives.

Themselves included.

As Lukas leads me into the security office, I stare at Rhylan standing at the helm of my station. I'm about to lose my temper when he sees me and backs away, holding out the datapad.

"Welcome back, Princess. If you'll permit me, I'll go over everything with you and then leave you to it."

The fact that he's ready to bow out without a fuss is a relief. I don't want to fight. Calli and Lukas both explained to me about his alpha selling him and his brother into servitude and how he was as much a victim as the rest of us under Laryssa's thumb.

I don't forgive him, but I'm starting to understand.

What I *don't* understand is how my brother fell in love with him. Creed is neither stupid nor easily swayed. If he mated this man, there must be more to him than I've seen in the dozen times I've run across him.

"I like the haircut," I say.

It sounds super stupid coming out of my mouth, but it's all I've got to offer him in the way of small talk. It's either that or 'Thanks for capturing me and returning me to my prison, asshole.'

I doubt that will help, so I go with the haircut.

The dragon reaches up to where the blond hair is shaved at the side of his head and shaggy and longer up top. "Thank you. New life. New look. You know?"

I hold out my hand for the datapad. "So, what have I missed?"

We spend the next hour going over Ruic Breard's empire, how he's financially tied with the other four supporters of the rebellion, and how he's connected with Hawk's half-brother.

"And you think the upsurge of public disturbances is them flexing their muscles?" I ask.

Rhylan shakes his head. "I think the rioters and street thieves are testing our response system and are planning something bigger."

"Bigger like what?"

"That we don't know."

"All right. What *do* we know?"

He outlines how the displaced citizens have been taken care of with Keyla's community outreach initiatives. We cover the new security measures he put in place to shut down the street bandits. The walk-in centers that Shadow and Dillan are organizing for physical and mental health in the aftermath of Laryssa's rule. And the plans for policing Creed's unveiling of the war memorial at the Dornte City Center tomorrow.

"Creed held off the unveiling, in the hopes you'd be able to join him in celebrating your parents. Shadow told him not to pressure you, but I know how much it would mean to him to have you there."

I'm not sure I'm ready to stand next to Creed, his child bride, my dragon prison guard, and their other mate at an event meant to commemorate my parents.

I can't imagine my parents would've approved.

"I'll think about it," I say, staring at the datapad and seeing nothing. "If you'll excuse me, I'm going to take this back to the suite and look it over there."

I don't wait for a response, because I don't care what he has to say. I make my exit and stride out into the hall and toward the stairs. I'm way too far from my suite and my emotions are coming unraveled.

Rhylan is doing my job... Keyla's outreach initiatives... Creed putting together the memorial for our parents... and I don't even know who Dillan is.

What the hell?

Lukas is tracking me, his long strides keeping pace with me with little effort. "Princess? What happened in there? Is everything all right?"

I crest the top of the stairs and my strength is flagging. I'm too tired for this. "I'm fine. Go back and work on things. I'm fine."

"Saying it twice doesn't make it true but if you want to pretend, I'll let you."

I ignore the jibe and walk the rest of the way in silence. When I round the corner toward the corridor that leads to the private residences, I nod at the guards at the door. "Gentlemen."

"Princess."

I step through the doors and despite my nerves being frayed, I manage to fake a calm smile.

Lukas is right behind me and with my weariness, my control on my mental energy is waning. It doesn't matter. All I need to do is get into my room and close my door and shut out the world.

One foot in front of the other, I make it to the end of the hall and figure I'm home free. Wrong. When I place my hand over the scanner, nothing happens.

Access denied.

I read the screen and it breaks my brain.

"Access denied?" I smack my hand against the screen. My palm stings but I do it again for good measure. "It's my *fucking* apartment! Let me in you stupid AI, piece of shit."

"Okay, easy." Lukas reaches around me and opens things up. "We'll reprogram that once we calm down. Laryssa likely had your access wiped when she ran the show. You were her prisoner, after all."

"Right. Thanks. I almost forgot."

When the door opens, I push through and storm straight into my room. Gripping the edge of the door, I swing it behind me and keep going, pulling my shirt up and over my head.

I'm halfway across the carpeted space when it registers that there was no slam. "Get out."

I don't even have to look back to know if he's there. I'm so wired I can feel him and all his sexual energy. As a mind guardian, it's normal to pick up the impulses of strong-minded people around me.

Normally, I can block it out.

Nothing is normal right now.

"Get out!"

"I'm getting out," he says, his voice rough. "I just wanted to say you don't have to do this on your own. I've been with you in this for almost two weeks. You don't have to front with me. If you need someone to hit or to hug or to scream at, I'm across the living room. Just be honest. You're not all right. Stop pretending you are and you'll be one step closer to reclaiming your power."

"Reclaiming my power?" My wings flare as my emotions hit in a wave of craziness. "What power? I'm tired, angry, and sad. I want to grab the reins of my life, but I don't know how because everything has changed, and I don't feel like this *is* my life anymore."

"That's not uncommon. I felt the same way when I got home from fighting overseas."

"But it's uncommon to me. Everyone's trying to help me and think for me and tell me how I should feel and I just want to be left alone for a damn minute."

He winks and dips his chin. "There you go. A good first step. You gotta let that shit out. Now, go crawl into bed and claim a few hours of rest. I'll make dinner for later and we'll see how you feel then."

Lukas

I close the door to Honor's room and put some distance between me and my impulse to follow the divining rod my dick thinks it is. Fuck me. In her bra and with those wings flaring out behind her, and her cheeks flushed with frustration, I nearly creamed my jeans.

She sucks the breath from my lungs.

How did that happen? I know the answer to that.

Spending the last two weeks lying beside her and navigating her unconscious plane formed a connection between us.

I didn't mean for it to happen, but it did.

The big question is whether or not she feels it because, as spectacular as she is, I won't pursue her and make a fool of myself if there's no interest on her end.

Shadow's right about that much.

She's been through enough and doesn't need me complicating things if she isn't into me.

Which I think she is.

I hope she is.

I roll my eyes and give myself an inward shake. Since when am I an unsure schoolboy?

I'm about to turn toward the kitchen when Calli and Shadow let themselves in.

"Hey there," Calli says. "What's new over here?"

I tilt my head toward the kitchen, and they follow. "We did a little physio this morning to build up her strength—"

"—Yeah, baby. And when you say physio, you mean..."

I peg Calli with a look. "I mean hand-to-hand sparring. She has frustrations and I thought it might do her good on two fronts to be able to punch it out."

"You didn't get too physical with her, did you?" Shadow asks.

I point to my lip which isn't as badly split and swollen as it was this morning but is still obviously injured. "I assure you, I took a few solid hits for the cause and let her burn off her frustration."

"Good man," Calli says, eyeing my lip. "So, where is she now? Can I visit?"

"Can you give her time to rest? We spent a couple of hours in the security room afterward and she used up her energy. She had a bit of a meltdown just now and went in to get some rest."

Calli nods. "No problem. I'll zip across the hall and take a nap myself. That way, I won't fall asleep on her later when we're visiting. Laters."

∼

Shadow

When Calli leaves, Lukas heads to the fridge and starts pulling out ingredients. "I'm not much of a cook but I can do one-pot meals like a freaking champion. I'm throwing this together for later. Do you want to eat with us? I'm sure you're anxious to spend time with her."

The *her* is obvious.

"I appreciate that. I'll be out for most of the day tomorrow with the memorial, so I would like to assess where the day has taken her. How have you found her?"

"Considering she's only been awake for twenty-four hours, I think she's doing fine. She's a little weaker than she'd like to admit, both physically and emotionally, but I've felt the mettle she's made of and that's temporary."

I watch as he tosses meat and vegetables and pasta indiscriminately into a pot. "What are you making?"

"My mother wasn't much of a cook. She used to invent things and call it a scary surprise. That's kind of how I approach cooking."

I laugh. "Scary surprise fails as a selling point for people to eat your meal."

"Maybe, but I've been told my scary surprise is amazing by more than one person."

My sister always says I am a foodie snob. I will reserve judgment on Lukas's cooking and prove her wrong. "Do you have the security details for the memorial tomorrow? I want to ensure it is safe but worry about it feeling like a police state event."

Lukas points toward the datapad on the table. "A visual presence of security and enforcers will not only make attendees feel safer, but it'll also deter any troublemakers from starting something."

"Do you think there will be trouble?"

"It's my job to anticipate that there will be and figure out how to mitigate the risk."

"Creed mentioned that there might be danger looming for Keyla. How accurate is that?"

"It's just a guess at the moment. There is chatter about taking 'Her' out. Keyla is the most recognizable female in Creed's camp and harming her would be the most direct way to bring him down."

I pull out a chair, swing it around to face me, and straddle the seat. Holding the datapad, I swipe a finger over the screen. "What are the orange triangles?"

"That's where Rhylan and I stationed backup teams at the recreation center and a few other out of sight locations. They won't engage unless there is a need."

"And the blue dots?"

"Those are where the Phoenix Quint and I will be stationed. Keyla will be with Creed and Honor. Rhylan and Doc will be part of our security teams keeping watch among the crowd."

I look at the layout and frown.

"You got something to say, Counsellor?"

"Nothing of any consequence. I simply wish these precautions weren't necessary."

"You and me both. The sad truth is they are."

Lukas sets his culinary abomination onto the back burner of the stove and sets it to simmer for the afternoon. I follow him out to the living area of the suite and hope the precautions remain unneeded.

Dornte has had enough trouble.

But, if Rhylan and Lukas think the added security is necessary to discourage more violence, I won't argue.

"Do you want a drink?"

"That would be welcome, yes."

He nods. "Perfect, give me one second to wash up and I'll be back to pour us something."

While he heads into his suite, I step onto the balcony and marvel at the grounds of Thornebane Castle. How can a place so beautiful be plagued with so much ugliness? The turmoil of the quadrant seems oddly out of place next to the rolling blue-green hills, the pink waters, and the two pastel moons.

I breathe deep and smile at the faint sweetness in the air. It's like the breeze carries a hint of vanilla on it.

It's so—*Ouch*—

I glare down at the bone dart sticking out of my chest. Before I can think... my knees buckle.

"Lukas!"

CHAPTER EIGHT

Lukas

I hear Shadow call my name and something about the pitchy tone of his voice sets off all kinds of alarm bells. Jogging out of my bathroom, I grab my gun from my shoulder holster lying on the desk and ease to the corner. A quick visual check around the corner and back tells me there is no one targeting me or approaching.

But there is an intruder.

A white-winged warrior with pointed ears and spiral horns is closing in on Honor's bedroom door. I pull back, tap the backup button on my watch and then take a breath.

In a rush, I move into the living room and position myself for a clean shot. "Not another step, fucker—"

The guy turns on me and it's on.

I fire, but barely get a shot off when he launches and flies across the space like a missile. Arms outstretched and talons bared, I'm momentarily taken back.

I manage to squeeze off two more rounds.

I'm expecting those white feathers to start bleeding red but no such luck. My shots don't seem to even be slowing him down.

There's a crash by the door and then I hear the roar of a pissed-off grizzly.

Excellent.

Brant is welcome in any fight.

It takes all I've got to strong-arm this guy far enough away from my throat to keep him from ripping me to shreds.

Those talons of his could do lethal damage.

It's jarring when he's ripped off me and thrown across the room. Brant pivots back from the birdman fling and offers me a hand to pull me to my feet.

Then, we get ready for the next wave.

The birdman catches himself mid-air and hovers before coming at me again.

Fuck... now there are two of them.

If the first guy's white feathers likened him to a snowy owl, the second guy is definitely a falcon.

And they are pissed.

Yeah, join the club.

As they launch into the air the second time, Brant's bear lets off a murderous roar and he launches in front of Calli. Not that anyone really needs to defend Calli, but she is pregnant, and we try to keep her safe.

Our phoenix may have arrived late to the party, but she catches up quickly. She bursts into flame and spreads her wings as a woman on fire.

Good thing she went that route because the ceiling height of this castle won't support her phoenix.

"Stop!" Honor's command rings loud and clear and the bird men stop their advance, close their wings, and turn to face her.

"Princess Honor." In unison, the two fall to one knee and press a fist against the rug.

Honor looks as stunned by the whole thing as we do.

"Friends of yours?" I pant, catching my breath.

"Amberloq warriors."

The two straighten to their full seven-foot height and press their shoulders back. "I am Tundra of the Snowy Peaks," the white one says, "and this is Dune of the Desert Planes. We answer your call, my queen. We are here to serve you."

Honor stares at them.

There's a moment of awkward silence and then Calli bursts out laughing. "Oh, girlfriend, you should see your face. If I wasn't on fire right now, I would *soooo* be taking pictures."

Honor blinks at her bestie and her mouth drops open. "Holy shit, you're like a human torch. Like that cartoon you used to watch."

"Firestar, yeah. Cool, eh?"

"No, hot," Brant says, waggling his brows. "Really, fucking hot."

Honor makes a face and then waves her hand in the air before her. "Okay, I've had enough of you like that. Extinguish yourself before you overcook your baby. You're freaking me out."

Calli shuts off her flames and heads toward the open door as naked as the day she was born.

"Why don't you have clothes on?" Honor asks.

She waves over her head, waggling her ass as she goes. "I haven't mastered that yet. It's still hit and miss."

"Definitely a miss, Calli girl." Honor takes a beat and then addresses the rest of us. "What happened? Who was shooting?"

I raise a finger in the air. "I heard Shadow cry for help and found the snowy owl man breaking into your bedroom. I called out for him to stop, and instead of listening or identifying himself, he flew across the room and attacked me."

"So, you tried to shoot him?"

I grunt. "A weird-ass birdman flew a million miles an hour at my face with his talons out. Yes, I tried to shoot him."

Brant chuckles. "I think we're glossing over the part where Shadow cried out for help? Is anyone worried or wondering about the elf?"

I look around the room and curse when I see the open door to the balcony.

Honor seems to follow my train of thought and leads the rescue. "Gods, you didn't throw him over, did you?"

Rushing outside, I'm both relieved and alarmed to find him lying in a heap on the stone floor on the far end of the balcony.

"Shadow? Are you all right?" Carefully, I roll him onto his back. There's a weird, tranq dart sticking out of his pec. I pull it free and pass it up to Honor.

"This wasn't necessary." Honor snaps.

I glance back at her. "Why does it sound like you know these two?"

"I don't, but I know *of* them. The Amberloq forces are largely made up of Elbirfae warriors… and since they came to me the moment you cleared the witch's curse, I assume they are two of my squadron generals."

They both nod.

The white one straightens and his wings flutter in the breeze behind him. "We are the sons of those who came before and are honored to dedicate ourselves to you, Princess."

Honor runs a hand over her face. "All right. So, this is happening. I can't say I'm surprised, but hey, it's been a day." She straightens, pushes back her shoulders, and lifts her chin. "Take a knee, gentlemen."

They do as she says without hesitation.

"I accept your oath of fealty and all that our joining implies. I welcome you."

The two men burst into a golden aura and Honor holds out her hand. The white feather guy presses his lips to her fingers. "I am yours to command for all the days and nights to come."

"I accept your oath, warrior."

Then the falcon birdman takes her other hand and kisses her fingers the same way. "I am yours to command for all the days and nights to come."

"I accept your oath, warrior."

The glowing aura that surrounded them creeps up her arms and spreads to outline her completely. Her wings burst out of her back and I gasp at the beauty.

She's too much.

But I am missing something important.

"What does your joining imply? What just happened? What does this mean?"

Creed steps onto the balcony and takes in the scene. "It means, Honor's destiny is at hand and her generals have claimed their place at her side. Long live the Guardian of the Crown."

～

Honor

As Creed says the words, it sinks in. I am the Guardian of the freaking Crown. It's something I've looked forward to my whole life just as he looked forward to being the king. My father and his sister should've run the quadrant as one as his father and sister did before them.

They didn't.

They fought and allowed personal feelings to affect the realm. I can't let that happen.

Creed is standing at the doorway looking tentative. I told him to keep his distance and here he is.

He frowns, and I know he's reading my energy. Holding up his hands, he offers me an apologetic smile. "Rhylan got Lukas's call for backup but isn't in the castle. I only meant to ensure your safety. I'll go. I'm sorry."

"No. *I'm* sorry," I say, blinking against the sting in my eyes. "We won't be like them."

He draws a heavy breath. "No. We won't."

I leave Shadow in Lukas's care and stride across the balcony and into Creed's hug. When he wraps his arms around me, the anger and suffering of the past two years lessen and the knot in my chest eases.

"There is only us now," I say, breathing him in. "We have to do better for Dornte than they did."

He squeezes the back of my head and kisses my cheek. "We will. Whatever it takes. Whatever you need."

I ease back and take a long look at him.

Last night when I woke up and he wanted to comfort me, I was overwhelmed by my suffering. Looking at him now, seeing these creepy ebony eyes that aren't his, knowing he just learned about our mother's death...

I realize how much he has suffered as well.

I take in our audience and decide not to dish up all our personal tragedies for the masses. "Brant, please check on Calli and tell her that even though I'll be busy for a couple of hours, I'll need to talk to her tonight and decompress."

The burly bear nods. "I'll tell her. I'm sure I am safe to accept on her behalf."

He leaves and I look at poor Shadow on the floor of the balcony. "Lukas, could you please help Shadow to the couch until he wakes up. I'm assuming it's only a sedative and nothing more lethal?"

I look to Tundra, and he dips his chin in agreement.

"Yes, Princess. We merely wanted to assess your situation and ensure your safety."

Lukas curses under his breath. "Did it occur to you to knock and say hello?"

I keep my focus on the two warriors and raise my hand to

cut off their answer. "I'm glad you're here. Come inside. There is so much we need to discuss."

Tundra

The woman is more beautiful than I imagined and my body thrums with anticipation. My Princess. My partner in life's destiny. *Mine.* As she speaks, I study the quirk of her mouth and watch the way she twists her fingers together in her lap. She is nervous.

That makes two of us.

Still, I feel the magic of our union vows taking hold.

I open the communication by trying to find a common interest between us. "Your aunt, Valorous, was a great and respected leader. May I express how deeply her death struck us all? From our hearts to our souls, we mourn her loss."

"Thank you, Tundra," King Creed says. "Can you tell us a bit more about what happened to the Amberloq and why they didn't respond when the realm needed them most?"

I bow my head. "The past years have been difficult, sire. Without Valorous's leadership, a great and fearsome power lost much of its strength. It is a tragedy that the once-proud organization was shattered to splinters."

Honor's expression softens. "She was an amazing woman. We mourn the loss as well. As for the fall of the Amberloq, I assure you that is temporary. Tell me, how many warriors remain?"

I press my palm to my chest. "I am ashamed to admit, I cannot say for certain. Before the outbreak of the skirmish here at the castle, the Amberloq stronghold was breached, and our numbers decimated. All members were either killed or so badly cursed that death was their only desire."

"Cursed how?" Creed asks. "How could so many warriors be taken down at once?"

"The Blood Witch invaded Valorous's chambers two days before Laryssa and her men invaded here and claimed the lives of your parents. They seized control of Valorous, and when the news spread, the natural response was for all those of able body to rush to her aid."

"It was a trap," King Creed says, his expression dour. "The witch lured the warriors in and then eliminated the quadrant's strongest defense."

I nod. "You are correct."

Princess Honor sighs and runs her hand through her lovely silver hair. "I always wondered why you didn't come to help. I knew Valorous was alive because I hadn't come into my powers, yet no one came to help us. For most of the first year, I wondered where you were."

"There was a great deal of chaos after the raids. In one devastating event, we went from numbering in the hundreds to be reduced to a handful."

She assesses me and then my desert brother. "And how did the two of you escape the raids?"

Dune drops his chin. "The week prior to the raids, we were involved in an altercation. The Amberloq are many bodies of one mind and one hand. To fight amongst ourselves is not tolerated."

"What is the punishment for the offense?" King Creed asks.

I meet his gaze and face his censure. "Those who have a falling from grace are sent to the Peak of Mount Nekko. It is a place of spiritual retreat used to allow warriors time and peace to come to a new understanding of how to work together."

Honor's eyes widen. "You two survived because you got into a brawl and were stuck on a mountain in a time out?"

He frowns. "I am sorry, Princess. You deserve finer warriors as your mates but sadly, we are that remain from our zones."

"Mates?" the military human says. "You said you are her generals. Now you're saying you're her mates?"

Honor looks at him and frowns. "Of course, they're my mates... or, they will be. They heard the call, they came, and I accepted their pledge."

The soldier looks from my princess to her brother and then to us. "Seriously?"

"That's our tradition," King Creed says. "Except there are supposed to be three—a representative from each of the biomes of the land—the desert plains, the snowy peaks, and the forested jungle."

The male frowns. "Three?"

Honor frowns at him. "Why is this upsetting you?"

The warrior clenches his jaw and exhales. "I'd have made more food if I knew your harem was arriving."

Dune

I don't know who this human is, but I don't like him. He acts like he has an interest in our private business—he doesn't. Tundra should've let me enter the princess's residence first. Then, at least, the male would be bleeding.

I sigh, casting a feather-fluttering look of warning.

Back off, she's ours.

As crazy as that is.

Who would've believed that *I* would end up the warrior general for the desert zone?

Not me.

Certainly not anyone who knows me.

Certainly not anyone who's ever met me.

Tundra's not much of a surprise. That guy is warrior

supreme and likely would've been called even if we weren't the only two Amberloq on the planet.

Yeah, Tundra's the kind of warrior that stands out. He thinks before he acts. He considers consequences. He's exactly the kind of political leader who should be mated to the Guardian of the Crown.

And that's exactly why I popped him one in his broody, arrogant face two years ago and saved our lives.

Of course, *he* doesn't think I saved our lives.

He thinks I deprived him of a chance to defend Valorous and robbed him of the honor of his duty.

Wrong.

The only thing I deprived him of was the chance to bleed out of his eye sockets and bodily liquify in a horrible mass murder.

He should be singing my praise and sucking my cock in thanks.

But no… I'm the one who messed up his life.

Hello? Aren't we the Generals of the Crown?

Yes, we are.

You're welcome.

"And you, Dune?" our lady asks. "Did many in your village survive?"

I meet her gaze and it feels like my breath is being sucked from my lungs. The purple of her eyes almost glows. "The women and children are well, of course. The desert zone has a dozen nomadic tribes and a few oasis villages. Nearly all men train to join the Amberloq, so after the Blood Witch attacked, that left me, as well as the old men who can barely get their wings up, and the fledglings who can barely keep their wings down."

Tundra rolls his eyes at me.

Lady Honor smiles.

See. Funny is charming.

"So, after two years, might there be young males who could

complete the ceremony of honor? Might there be a new generation of warriors available to train?" she asks.

"A handful, maybe. Not a force like we were though, I'm afraid."

"What does this ceremony of honor entail?" the human asks, diverting our conversation. "Is it an actual test of your abilities? Is it like a military boot camp?"

The vein at the side of Tundra's head is pulsing.

That's never a good sign. Thankfully, I'm not the one annoying him most at the moment.

"I assure you, human, our ceremony of honor is a true test. To stand at the side of the Guardian of the Crown and defend the quadrant is a great honor. It is something to be earned."

He arches a dark brow, his skepticism thinly veiled. "Earned? Says the warrior chosen to be the general of his biome by default?"

Tundra's back muscles twitch and his feathers ruffle. *Oh, dumb human. You shouldn't have said that. Tundra will carve you open while you sleep.*

I fight to keep a straight face.

As much fun as it is to torment Tundra, it's even more fun to watch another person tick his boxes because I won't be the one breathing out my ass later when he twists me into a knot.

Much more fun for me.

King Creed seems to pick up on Tundra's annoyance and offers the human a patient smile. "Lukas is the male who took down Laryssa for us and was instrumental in us finding Honor and bringing her back from the Blood Witch's curse. Without him, my sister wouldn't be freed from her catatonic state, and you wouldn't have activated as Amberloq Generals."

Huh... "But he's human, right?"

Honor nods. "A human warrior from the Human Realm. He is also a mage... which is *not* a witch."

Lukas meets the gaze of our queen and something private and playful passes between them.

No. No. No. That won't do. Why would she consider him? He doesn't even have wings. He doesn't get to have private looks with our princess.

I glance down at Tundra's fingers and smile. His talons are out in full extension.

Tundra doesn't like the familiarity either.

Get your own princess, human. This one is ours.

I'm still staring him down when his watch lets off a quiet beep. He lifts it to examine and frowns. "If you'll excuse me. Duty calls."

King Creed and Princess Honor both stand.

"Is it something we should be aware of?" Creed asks.

"Rhylan's search into hostile opposition to your rule dug something up and he wants my opinion. You two go ahead and finish with your meet and greet. I'll be back as soon as I can. Dinner is on the stove. We can catch up when I get back."

The male retreats into the bedroom on the opposite side of the suite and returns a moment later wearing a shoulder sheath. Before he leaves, he steps over to the table against the wall and collects his weapon.

"If it's simply your opinion the dragon wants, why do you need your gun?" Honor asks.

The man lifts one shoulder and winks. "You never know when you might have to start shooting at intruders. It's best to be prepared."

Tundra chuffs. "Not that your metal pellets did any damage. Anyone with a bit of body armor will still have the upper hand."

"Okay then," Honor says, walking the human to the door. "I'll expect a full report when you get back. And, as always, Lukas... thank you."

He offers her a private smile. "And, as always, you're welcome, Princess."

CHAPTER NINE

Shadow

I wake in a strange bed with a throbbing hangover beating like a war drum in my head and Lukas asleep in the bed next to me. There's nothing sexual about it. He's fully dressed, other than his feet, and looks like he simply got in late and crashed onto the mattress.

That explains him being here.

Why am I here? And why do I feel like I drank elderberry wine all night and did something stupid?

Being careful not to wake Lukas, I roll off the side of the bed and spend a moment in the washroom. Grabbing a cloth, I wash my face with cold water and press it on my face. That helps clear the cobwebs a little.

I lean on the vanity as the world spins in a slow circle around me and try not to lose my balance and crack my head on the marble counter. Checking myself in the mirror, I assess the damage.

I don't look like I was out drinking all night.

The last thing I remember is…

A rush of nausea hits me so hard my vision expands to black. On a blind lurch, I drop and grapple for the toilet. The impact of my knees cracking against the tile of the floor vibrates up to my hips but I'm too busy to worry about it as my stomach revolts.

I heave forward, the acid bite of vomit and bile burning the back of my throat.

What the hell did I eat? Drink? Do?

A rush of feverish sweats hit, and my entire body starts to shake.

"Okay, shit," Lukas says, rushing in. "Are you all right?"

"Not even a little." My body tightens and then I retch again.

Lukas gathers my hair and pulls it back which is kind but odd. When the next round of ejection ends, I lay my arms around the seat of the toilet and rest my head on my arm. "Am I drunk?"

"No. You're drugged."

"Drugged? By whom?"

Lukas releases my hair and I close my eyes. A moment later, he presses a cold cloth against my forehead once more. "While you were on the balcony, two birdmen flew up, shot you with a tranq dart, and proceeded to insert themselves into Honor's life."

"Who are they?"

"From what I've been told, the Guardian of the Crown binds herself to the leaders of the three biomes of the quadrant. Each quadrant gets a representative and they become a unit, much like Calli and her mates."

"And they showed up and shot me for no reason?"

"I think it was bad timing on your part to go out for fresh air when you did. They said they came to assess her situation."

"And what's wrong with knocking on the door?"

Lukas grunts. "Exactly my question. They defended their

choice and said they had no way of knowing if Honor was here and safe or remained a prisoner."

I grunt. "Except that Creed has made several public appearances announcing that Honor is safely home and in his care."

Lukas holds up his hands. "I'm just the messenger. I thought it was overkill, too."

I test the state of unrest churning in my belly and figure I am ready to give up my current position of worshiping the porcelain god. After another pass of the cold cloth over my face and forehead, I get to my feet and flush the toilet.

Standing might be a mistake.

I close the lid and take a seat, dropping my head towards my lap. "Did you say birdmen?"

"Well, more a cross between angels and devils. Elbirfae, they're called. I looked them up. They've got full-height wings that give them a fifteen-foot wingspan, pointed ears like elves, horns like demon goats, and apparently, they tend to lead the Dornte defense team."

"They sound like powerful warriors."

"Who shot an innocent guy with a tranq dart for no reason."

I feel like a sock tumbled too long in the dryer, but there is too much to do to stay in here all day. "What time is it?"

"Just past seven."

I scrub my hands over my face and shake myself awake. "All right. I shall return to my room for another hour of sleep and then get ready to head over to prepare for the memorial. Are you coming with the king and his mates later?"

He nods. "Yeah. The SUVs came through yesterday afternoon. I'll be part of the caravan."

"Fine. I'll see you there."

Getting my feet to cooperate with my decision to leave takes a moment, but eventually, I make my way out of Lukas's guest suite and into the living room.

Glancing over at the two large warriors sleeping on the

couches it's a little unnerving how much of those couches their warrior frames consume.

And wow, they really do look like birdmen.

When I look at them, something within me awakens in recognition. They have elven blood in them and I can sense it. I study the beautifully sculpted men with feathered wings. Other than their tipped ears, I would never have pictured them as part elves.

Interesting.

I'm about to let myself out when Honor exits her bedroom. When she sees me, she signals for me to follow her down the hall toward the kitchen.

When we get there, she turns around hugs me. "I'm so sorry you got caught in the crossfire craziness of my life. Are you all right?"

"I shall do." Yes, it is a lie but there is nothing to be gained by making her feel worse than she already does. "Lukas told me what happened. Are *you* all right? Having two strangers show up with expectations must be daunting, especially after the past few years."

She seems to think about that and then shrugs. "The opposite, really. I've understood my duty as Guardian of the Crown and how that would play out since I was a kid. After the uncertainty of my time in captivity, I find it reassuring. I'm looking forward to moving forward."

That is not the answer I expected but the thing about being a good counselor is allowing my patients to find their own paths. "And how do you feel about the part of the arrangement that introduces them as your mates?"

Again, she seems thoughtful in her consideration of my question. "They are both good-looking, strong men who seem to respect their duties and care about their zone representation. I respect that. They are also age-appropriate and have been courteous to me."

"That is more a description of their character than your feelings about sharing your heart and your bed with them."

She chuckles. "You're reading too much into it, Shadow. Being bound to the zone generals is a political alignment more importantly than a romantic one. If my aunt taught me one thing, it's that I decide who I love. I don't feel any pressure to give these men my heart. They are here for a purpose, as am I. We are servants of Dornte and our first responsibility is the stability of the crown. If that becomes more, then I'll deal with it then."

Not knowing much about the traditions of the realm, it's difficult to comment on that effectively. She does, however, seem to be content with the idea.

That is a relief.

"Have you given any thought to joining the celebration of life at the war memorial later today? I know you and your brother have issues to work through but—"

"Oh, you missed that. Creed was here all of yesterday afternoon and we worked through everything—well, at least on a political front and as siblings. I'm still not pleased with his choice of mates, and he's not pleased with my opinion, but as far as he and I go, we're good."

"So, you plan to be at the memorial?"

"Definitely. Creed and I will both say a few words and hopefully, reassure the citizens Dornte is through the troubled times and there is only peace and happiness ahead."

"I am pleased to hear that, Princess."

She tilts her head and chuckles. "Why don't I believe you, Shadow?"

I feel the heat of a blush warming my ears and offer her an apologetic smile. "After all you've been through, it is quite all right if you're not one-hundred percent pieced back together. Grief and trauma are tricky things. My reluctance stems from my concern that you have been through a lot, both mentally and physically, and have not yet had the time to deconstruct those emotions."

"I feel the tension in your words and by the mental energy you're giving off, I think I know why. There are things about mind guardian fae you might not be aware of. Because we sense and take on the emotional energy of those around us, we can isolate traumatic memories and emotions and remove them."

"Remove them? You mean you don't remember what happened?"

"No, I do. I remember being assaulted by Laryssa's guards and by the drow mercenaries who killed my host body. I remember it but the emotional connection to the event is no longer a part of who I am. I discharged it."

"I've never heard of this."

"You are new to the Fae Realm."

"That is true… and if you are right, I am truly happy for you. Still, if you need to process and want someone to talk to, I am available."

She reaches forward and hugs me once again. "I spent what amounts to ten years with Calli. I have dealt with everything that needs to be addressed. I think you'll find I'm so well-adjusted I'm boring."

"I honestly hope you are right, and I am not needed. It would be my greatest pleasure to be bored by you."

Honor

I walk Shadow out and then examine the two warriors overflowing on the couches in my living room. They refused to leave me last night and take another suite. With Lukas here, things are getting crowded. It looks like it's time to evaluate the state of Amberloq Hall.

Valorous had the private military residence shut up and closed down almost two decades ago, but technically, it's ours to claim.

It's hard to believe I initiated a union with these two glorious males. Where Lukas is wiry-fit, my generals are built like gladiators. An image further accentuated by them not wearing shirts.

Their muscled shoulders and chiseled pecs and abs are barely hidden by the leather battle vests they wear.

And how sexy is that?

I swallow and admire Tundra's pale complexion and ebony hair as well as Dune's warm, brown skin and sandy blond hair.

And those horns... I'm so drawn to stroke them and see what they feel like.

The sound of water running draws me through the living room to Creed's old room. Lukas came in later than I expected last night, and I had already given up on hearing what Rhylan found and gone to bed.

I'm curious to learn what happened after he left.

Realm security, after all, is within my purview, and as soon as I'm completely recovered, I'm taking it back from him and Rhylan.

I sigh. If I'm being honest with myself, a larger part of my reason for needing to see Lukas is because I didn't like the way he left yesterday.

He was obviously put out by Dune and Tundra.

He and I have been hot and flirty, but I didn't peg him for the kind of guy to get territorial over a female he hasn't even kissed yet.

I let myself into his bedroom and close the door behind me. Climbing onto the bed I laugh. Both Shadow and Lukas crashed in here last night and yet the bed is still made.

Don't men get *into* bed?

I guess it's manlier to be on the bed if you have to share with another dude.

Even if that dude is drugged and unconscious.

Stretching out on top of the comforter, I cross my feet, look up at the ceiling, and wonder about things. How did Creed survive two years of Laryssa and the dragons? At least I escaped for a year, so I had a respite.

My brother never got that.

Maybe Lukas can break his curse like he did mine?

I close my eyes and let my thoughts drift. If things in life happened as they are meant to, what am I meant to do next? If Tundra and Dune are the only Elbirfae warriors who survived the Blood Witch's attack, how do I rebuild the Amberloq?

The water shuts off and I roll onto my side and prop my head up with my hand.

Naked, towel, or dressed?

How does Lukas roll? Men are generally creatures of habit, so I wonder how the next few minutes will play out. I'm hoping naked but will take what I can get.

The click of the door latch signals his exit from the bathroom. He rides the crest of a rush of steamy, humid air and at first, I'm disappointed.

Not naked.

He's wearing a pair of tight, black boxers and has a towel hanging around his neck. With his head down and his hand scrubbing over his dark hair, he doesn't notice me until he's almost to the bed.

I expect him to startle or at least look surprised. He doesn't. The side of his mouth curls up at the side.

"Hello, Princess... something I can do for you?"

The husky purr in his voice ignites all kinds of ideas of things he can do for me. "I wanted to check in with you. Find out what you were up to last night. Is there anything I should know about?"

He finishes with the towel and steps past me to hang it over the back of the chair. The side trip gives me a glorious view: the clench and release of his muscled back, the corded muscles of his thick thighs, the perfect form of his tight ass...

He catches me checking him out and chuckles. "Anything you should know about on a professional level or personal?"

"Professional, of course. Rhylan had concerns. What were they about?"

"The dragon unraveled a few significant threads of conversation using Laryssa's spyware algorithm he's got running. There are a few very disgruntled one-percenters that don't want your brother in power."

"Do we have anything specific we can act on?"

"Not yet, but we're back at it this morning."

"Am I holding you up?"

He walks over to the edge of the bed and looks down at me, his ebony brow arched. "Even if you were, Rhylan would have to wait."

Good answer.

"Then you have a moment to spare to help me with a favor?"

"What do you need?"

I sit up, grab the hem of my silk cami and pull it over my head. His eyes light up as a sexy smile brightens his face. "I like favors that start like this."

I waggle my eyebrows, roll onto my stomach, and sweep my hair over my shoulder. "Either I laid unconscious too long or we tweaked something during our workout yesterday, but something is out of whack with my back. If you don't mind helping a girl out."

He chuckles and takes my silk top to hang it on the handle of the bedside table. "Do you have any massage oils for me to use?"

"Maybe in Creed's bathroom?"

"One moment, I'll see what I can find." He's back a moment later with a bottle in his hand. The mattress dips beneath his weight as he climbs up beside me. "Now, where is this out of whack issue?"

"Feel around. I have no doubt you'll find it. And take your time. I have a lot of kinks to work out."

"Kinks, eh? Good to know. I'm all for kinks." The moist friction of palms rubbing together precedes Lukas's hands fanning out on my shoulder blades.

I close my eyes and absorb his ministrations. This wasn't a coy seduction, my back *is* aching and sore... and my oh my the mage has a gift.

"Oh, yeah," I breathe, endorphins releasing all through my body. "That's perfection."

Lukas's hands are strong, his fingers kneading over the knots and kinks of months of captivity and neglect. "Tell me if the pressure's too much and I'll ease up."

"No," I gasp, a little too eagerly. I swallow, embarrassed that my voice is far too thready to hide my state of ecstasy. "Don't change a thing. This is perfect. Do you mind if I take advantage of your magic fingers for a while longer?"

"As long as you like, Princess, but I'd have a better position if I straddled your ass."

I close my eyes, gripping my fingers into the soft cushion of my comforter. "You do you, Mr. Mage."

He shifts and a moment later his knees frame my hips and he's hovering over my ass. Damn, having him centered over my body dials me up another notch.

Maybe this wasn't a good idea.

"These ridges here," he says, caressing the three-inch cartilage lines that run parallel to my spine. "This is where your wings come out?"

I swallow, pressing my forehead into the blankets. My spinal ridges are incredibly sensitive, and Lukas is rubbing them in all the right ways.

"Yes. That's where my wings come out... and FYI, those

ridges are a major erogenous zone for fae females. You're basically rubbing me off right now."

The deep-throated chuckle is *waaaay* too sexy. "And is that okay with you or should I stop?"

"Please, don't stop," I pant, my breath quickening, "but there's a very real chance I'm going to cream myself if you continue."

"Then there's no way I'm stopping. This time when I get you off, I intend to be in the same room."

I chuckle, too far gone to try to deny what happened on the dream plane two nights ago. "I didn't mean for that to happen."

"It was fine... better than fine. I think after what you've been through you deserve all the orgasms you can get and I'm volunteering to give them to you."

Yeah, well, he's about to.

"Do you mind if I..." I'm trying to ask if it will put him off if I touch myself, but my mind is scattered.

I can't think. All I can manage is to feel.

And oh... it feels so good.

"Whatever you need, Honor. My answer is yes."

Man, his voice is a husky rasp and with that accent... I raise my hip, slide my hand beneath the elastic of my baby doll shorts, and sink my fingers into the moisture of my core.

"Oh, gods." I close my eyes and groan as sensation builds in delicious waves.

"That's it, Princess. How good does this feel?"

I moan as he massages over everything that aches and then leans forward to tongue those two ridges. His kiss is probing, his teeth grazing the ridges as the light stubble of his chin brushes over the sensitive flesh.

"How wet are you right now, Honor?"

"So wet."

"Sink your fingers inside and give your pussy something to grip onto. I'm going to make you come hard and it'll feel better if you're filled. Remember, I've got you. Whatever happens next, just trust me."

I'm about to ask what he means when something delicious and warm tingles through my insides.

It's my sexy shadow.

It's Lukas's magic inside me, coaxing me toward my release. He nips one of my spinal ridges and I cry out, consumed by pleasure.

"Come for me, Princess. Let yourself fall."

Light explodes behind my eyelids as my hips buck and I wish I had something more substantial than my fingers to ride.

Doesn't matter.

My eyes roll back into my head, and I pant through the convulsions of the pull and release. The orgasm is sharp and lasts for ages. I have no doubt that it's Lukas's magic that draws out my pleasure.

I don't care.

This is the best I've felt in years.

Who am I kidding? This is the best I've ever felt.

CHAPTER TEN

Tundra

I wake to the throaty, feminine moans of a woman being pleasured—generously pleasured, by the sound of things. It makes sense now... the soldier's preoccupation with our worthiness. The male is involved with Lady Honor.

"Is that...?" Dune abruptly sits up on the opposite couch. "Are they...?"

I sit up as well and stretch out my wings. "They are definitely doing something, and it sounds like he is honoring her commendably."

Dune frowns at me. "Shake your feathers, that's our female in there and that human is having sex with her."

I stand and stretch my neck from side to side. "Honor Thornebane is the Guardian of the Crown. We are her generals and that means whatever *she* decides it means: perhaps lovers, perhaps military support, perhaps friends fighting a common purpose. She is our queen."

Despite being one of the most talented sword fighters I've ever seen, the boy from the desert planes is irreverent, driven by his emotions, and a maverick. He thinks his proficiency in melee battle entitles him to things above other people.

Like being a Crown General.

Like being the mate of our queen.

He scowls at me. "So, what? You're good with him in there polishing his staff with a rough buff and grind?"

I strike out with my wing and snap him in the shoulder. "Watch your mouth. When you disrespect what's going on in the privacy of that bedroom, you disrespect both of them and I won't have you shaming our queen."

He rolls his eyes. "You're a better male than me then because it pisses me off."

"I am definitely a better male than you and it's about time you realized it. The people of the tundra understand that to take pleasure with another is a gift, not a right. Even if our queen sparks a fondness for us, she will only ever be ours if that's what *she* chooses."

"Slecking hell, ice prince, if that's the way you look at things it's no wonder you're a middle-aged virgin."

Now it's my turn to roll my eyes. "You can make up any lies you like, but what I say is true. Only after you learn to respect a lover will you create a binding relationship with one."

"Do you spend a lot of time in the sacred temples? I swear half the crap that comes out of your mouth is happy-happy rhetoric from the fae priests."

In the human's bedroom, our queen's pleasures climax, and then the feminine sounds crescendo.

Good for her. From what we learned yesterday, she has suffered and deserves to be pleasured.

I point to my travel bag on the floor. "If our queen wonders where I am, I'll be in the guest bathroom down the hall readying for our day."

Dune gives me a sidelong look and points to my groin.

"Which is your stick-up-the-ass way of saying you're hard and need to stroke off."

"No. It's not. You're a disrespectful idiot."

The bastard moves in a blur and bumps my chest as he palms the front of my trousers. His hand strokes over the fabric of my pants, the pressure rubbing the stiff column of my erection. "Maybe, but I'm right."

Chest-to-chest there's a moment's hesitation when his hand is working up and down my length. It's a natural reaction to respond to such stimuli. It's perfectly understandable.

His mouth quirks up in a cocky grin.

I almost don't want to push him away... but I do.

I shove him off and turn away, grabbing my bag off the floor as I go. Without stopping, I stride down the hallway and shut myself into the powder room. Gripping the edge of the marble vanity, I lean forward and try to breathe through my arousal.

It's bad enough that I was aroused by the thought and sound of Honor having sex with the human soldier.

It's worse that Dune realized it...

It's much worse that I responded to his touch.

I stare down at the fabric peak in my pants and curse. There's no way I'm finishing what Dune started.

It's wrong.

It's embarrassing.

It's exactly what I need to do or I'll never be able to focus today.

The latch of the door flips into place with a heavy *click* and then I pull my trousers down my muscled thighs. Glancing around at where best to do this, I perch my ass against the cold, marble countertop.

With one hand on my cock and the other massaging the sac below, I take matters into my own hands.

Slecking Dune.

This is his fault.

~

Shadow

When my alarm goes off, I spend a few extra moments lying in the darkness listening to the sounds of Thornebane Castle. This place is very different from the Prime Palace back in the Human Realm. When you listen here, the rooms are quiet. At the palace, it doesn't matter when you listen or where you are, there's always a distant hum of activity.

For an elf with heightened hearing, that's tiring.

For a dark oracle hybrid that's excruciating.

Not that anyone knows about my dark oracle side. Thankfully, my father's physical traits are dominant, and I've never manifested any of the traits of my mother or her people.

That means I can live as an elf with no one any the wiser and without needing to explain.

I shower and dress for the memorial ceremony, and then double-check my datapad to see if Rhylan or Keyla have any last-minute instructions. The only new message from the queen is that there will be food before we leave.

Lovely. I gather what I need for the day, pack my hip satchel, and after a quick, half-cup of coffee, step outside my room and—

"Morning, counselor," Lukas says, coming out of the heirs' suite with Honor and the two feathered fae generals behind him. He steps across the hall and knocks twice against the door of the Amber Suite with the side of his fist. "Ready for the big event, Shadow?"

Since I met Lukas several weeks ago, there has never been a moment where I considered him upbeat. He is courteous, succinct, extra-ordinarily good at his job, but never has he walked with a bounce in his step and a light in his hazel green eyes.

Until today.

I sigh. Even if I wasn't trained to read emotional cues and body language, my heightened senses would pick up that these two are sexually charged and highly attracted to one another.

Not only did the man *not* heed my request to respect Honor's healing and recovery, but the two of them are forming an emotional bond that complicates her destiny with her generals.

What a wonderful start to our day.

The procession stops in front of me, and Honor and her generals turn to greet Calli and the quint.

Lukas looks at me and shakes his head. "Careful, Elf. Today's a big day. Don't ruin it by overthinking things you have no say in."

Right. Why overthink? Why not simply let life unfold on a whim and a wonder?

Ignoring everything I wish I could say to him, I shift my gaze to Honor and wait until the good mornings have ceased. "Princess, you look lovely. Shall we head to the King's Tower? I believe your brother and his mates are waiting for us there."

Honor offers me a smile. "Then let's not keep them waiting."

The ten of us make a loud and rowdy group as we travel the corridors of Thornebane Castle.

Calli rushes to the front of the pack to link her arms with Honor and the two of them start chatting privately.

Hawk and Brant move forward to walk with Lukas and they start a conversation about concerns for the day.

Jaxx and Kotah engage the two new members of the crew in polite conversation.

It makes me smile that the Wolf King, the leader of our realm is kind and genuine enough to make small talk with strangers.

It strikes me that I am the odd man out.

That is nothing new, but still, one of these days I should like to be included in the easy conversation of friends. My father used to say that unconsciously, others could sense the 'other' of my mother's genetics at work. Oracles are known to be solitary beings—dark oracles even more so.

Still, one day I would like to *not* be alone.

I try not to dwell on that because Honor is a mind guardian and can sense the mental energy of others. I was asked here to counsel her on putting the past to rest. How would it look if I am the one with personal issues?

~

Honor

As we travel the halls of the castle, the distance between the King's Tower and our suite strikes me with a pang of regret. The royal residence in the King's Tower is huge. Creed and I could've lived with our parents right until the end.

They didn't like the idea of us being so far away from them, but Creed and I wanted to step out of their shadow and live 'on our own.'

Or at least, that's what we told them.

Mostly, we wanted to drink, party, and have lovers not freak out about getting caught in the walk of shame by the king and queen of the realm.

In hindsight, I would've rather stayed with them and not lost out on the time we missed.

"Good morning, all," Creed says, opening the door as we arrive. "Come in. We have a buffet breakfast prepared so we can eat while we go over the final details of the day to come."

I stop to hug him good morning as the rest of the troop passes by.

"Mimosas, anyone?" the tall blond cowboy asks. That one is Jaxx. The Texan EMT jaguar shifter, I'm pretty sure. The group merges in a round of smiles and welcome and then spread out with a familiarity that suggests they've spent a great deal of time here.

I've missed so much.

Calli hugs Keyla and her brother, Kotah, leans in to kiss her forehead. It's all so domestic.

"The quint seems very comfortable here," I say.

"Of course," Creed says, smiling at the crowd. "They're family."

There's not an ounce of hesitation or reserve in his statement.

"They're Keyla's family," I correct.

His smile tightens. "No. They may have started as Keyla's family, but the way they love and support one another, they soon adopted me and Rhy as part of the clan. We are all family."

"Uh-huh."

"Honor, it doesn't have to be us versus them."

"That's not what I'm saying."

He arches a brow. "Isn't it? It's very obvious you don't approve of Keyla or Rhylan and you've never even introduced yourself to Dillan."

"I've only been awake for two days."

"And you visited Calli and the quint for a drink last night after everything settled down. How do you think that makes me and my mates feel?"

Shit. "I'm sorry. I wasn't ready to smile and play the one happy family game."

"But we *are* one happy family," he says. "The minute I was bound to Keyla, Kotah and the quint considered me family. Dillan was already in Keyla's heart and brother to Brant. Rhylan and I were a bit of a jumbled mess, but it was Keyla who recognized what we could be first and pulled us together. It was also Keyla's place in my life that brought about Calli figuring out you were her Riley."

I check over my shoulder to ensure our conversation is private and frown. "We don't need to talk about this."

"I think we do."

"Here? Now?"

"Do you think they don't know how you feel? Kotah is an omega and Keyla is highly empathic. Rhylan and the other wildlings can smell your frustration and mistrust. Calli is the only one who might not be aware and that's only because her mates go out of their way not to upset her, especially with the pregnancy."

Damn. I thought I'd been more subtle.

"All right. It bothers me that our realm is in turmoil, and you mated a child."

He doesn't look a bit surprised. "And when you take five minutes to speak with her, you'll realize you're being unfair. Today at the memorial step back and watch how she interacts with the citizens. I guarantee you, the universe got everything right."

I run my fingers over my hair and flick my braid to rest on my back. "I hear what you're saying but I can't talk about this right now. I'm not ready to get into emotions. I want to focus on our parents and the security for the event."

Creed nods. "That's fine. I told you I'll give you the time you need, and I meant it. I just wanted to be straight with you, so you know you're not fooling anyone."

"Awesome, thanks."

He gestures to the great room and steps toward the gathering of family and friends. "Come inside. I had the place remodeled a few weeks ago to eradicate any sign of the bitch queen. I think Mom and Dad would've liked how things turned out."

~

Lukas

As Rhylan and I go over the security plan with everyone one last time, I try not to stare at Honor and Creed talking privately in the hall. Normally, I'd say there would be no privacy in a room full of wildlings, but with the noise of all of us and the clatter of plates and cutlery and chatter, I doubt anyone will overhear what's going on.

Creed doesn't look happy.

For a brief moment, I wonder if he has somehow learned about our morning activities. He wouldn't care, would he? Well, of course he would care—Honor's his sister—but I don't think he'd be angry.

She's a grown woman and he likes me.

I nod at something Hawk is saying and my gaze falls back on Honor. She looks lovely. She didn't want to be in a dress and heels in case trouble breaks out so chose silver slacks with a navy-blue fitted bodice that spills down into a skirt that splits open at the front and back.

It's striking and looks amazing with her hair.

"And so, I thought naked and wearing only my gun holster is the way to go. Right, Lukas?"

I nod. "Yeah, Jaxx. That sounds about right."

Brant snorts and tilts his head into my line of sight. "Earth to Lukas. You just permitted him to attend the event with his junk on display."

"It seems our boy is distracted," Hawk says, grinning like an ass. "Could this sudden show of emotion have anything to do with you two smelling like eau de female orgasms?"

I roll my eyes. "Fuck off."

They all start to chuckle.

"I'm serious, you guys. Shut your mouths or I'll shove my Glock up your ass and blow your head off."

That only makes them laugh harder.

Hawk waves his hand to cut off the ribbing as the birdmen step over to join us with heaping plates of food. "And we'll have to keep our comms open at all times. If Hunter got together with the goblin for either revenge or a contingency plan, the quadrant's memorial celebration will be a prime opportunity to wreak havoc."

Shadow frowns. "Do you think that's likely? We're expecting a crowd of thousands today."

Rhylan meets the elf's question with a sigh. "Yes, something will likely happen. If not Hunter and Ruic, then some disgruntled follower of Laryssa's who enjoyed the military state and fear-mongering. Watch for gangs of street bandits. They travel in packs and love to cause trouble."

"How will we know if we see them?" Jaxx asks.

"They're mouthy skinheads with war paint and grunge clothes," Keyla says. "You can't miss them. They think they're tough but mostly they intimidate and rob innocent people."

Doc grins. "Taking out the three that tried to rob our bus was the most fun I've had since I've been here."

"Thanks a lot," Rhylan says. "That doesn't say much for your mates entertaining you, does it?"

The bear laughs as his cheeks go pink. "I meant the most PG public fun I've had since I've been here."

"Better," Keyla says, chuckling. "Much better."

Once we've gone over the layout of the Dornte City Center and the team assignments a few times, I dismiss everyone to enjoy their breakfast.

"You've got twenty minutes, people. Eat, piss, and be ready to roll. Oh, and take it easy on the mimosas—Jaxx, I'm looking at you, Jaguar."

CHAPTER ELEVEN

Dune

Ａfter we all stuff our bellies in the King's Tower, we waddle as a group to the back of the castle, where three black trucks wait for us. It seems King Creed has imported a squadron of fighters from the Human Realm.

Which, I found out yesterday afternoon, includes the legendary Phoenix and her Guardians. I study the sassy blonde who apparently was born human and resurrected as a wildling savior.

Yesterday when she faced off against us, she was slecking magnificent.

She doesn't look like much right now.

Well... other than her tits. Big. Full. I like the way they bounce when she walks. Yeah, I could bury my face in those mounds and take a nap.

Or better yet. I could bury my—

The rumbling growl of a jungle cat rattles in my chest. I track the sound back to the sandy-haired mate glaring at me with glowing turquoise eyes. "How 'bout you stick those eyeballs back in your noggin' and mind your own female, birdman."

Tundra stops walking and waits while we catch up. "Is there a problem, Jaxx?"

"Oh, no problem. I'm happy to teach your falcon friend here what it means to play the part of the cat toy of a jaguar."

I frown at the accusing look on Tundra's face. "I didn't do anything."

"Not unless you count fantasizing about my mate and undressin' her with his eyes while throwin' off the stench of arousal."

Tundra looks at me and scowls. "You can't possibly be that stupid."

I shrug and hold my hands up. "Maybe take it as a compliment. She's an attractive female and bound to be noticed."

"Noticed is fine," the massive grizzly man says, joining the conversation. "Ogled and objectified is a different story. Heed Jaxx's warning, General. You won't get more than one."

Jaxx snaps his teeth at me and lets off another long growl. "Or ignore the warning and I'll be spittin' feathers for a week."

Tundra grabs my wing and pulls me away from the truck. "You boys take the conveyances. We'll fly overhead and provide air support and surveillance. Sorry to have offended you, gentlemen."

Jaxx nods his chin, his gaze half-hooded.

The members of our party divide into groups and climb into the trucks. The four males of the Phoenix Quint get in the first truck.

Rhylan climbs into the driver's seat of the second truck and King Creed, Lady Keyla, and their bear doctor mate join him.

And then the human climbs behind the wheel of the third truck and Honor, Calli, and the elf join him.

As the line of black vehicles pulls away, Tundra gives me one last glare. "Try not to offend the most powerful people in our realm."

I chuff. "It wasn't that bad. And who knew he would be able to smell my mood?"

"He's a wildling. *Everyone* knows they have heightened senses."

"Oh, well, fine. No more fantasizing about sticking my face in the blonde woman's cleavage."

Tundra gapes. "And why would you be? Yesterday we became Honor's generals. She accepted our claim and initiated the joining. We have our own beauty to admire."

I push off the ground and spread my wings, pumping to increase my lift and follow the line of trucks. "Then she spent the morning sexing with the human."

"We don't know what they were up to."

I snort. "We've got a fairly good idea."

"That is their business."

"So, what? She already has something going on with the human so we wait in line?"

Tundra makes a face. "I swear, if we were on the ground, I'd smack you. Honor is a person, not our property. Her trust and her affection need to be earned."

"We're her generals—the male representatives of the quadrant biomes. What more is there to know?"

He lets off a long, suffering sigh. "Honor will strike the balance of how things unfold. But I'll give you a hint. If you're ogling her best friend, who is also the wife of four other men, and also pregnant with their child, you're slitting your own throat."

As much as I hate to admit it, I see his point. "All right. That was stupid… wait… *pregnant?*"

He looks at me like I'm an idiot… which is pretty much how he always looks at me. "Yes, the phoenix is pregnant and carries the young of her mates. Did you not notice the round of her belly?"

"No. I was more interested in the rounds of her tits."

"Try to be more observant and less crass. Yes, she is months pregnant and it's likely another reason why they are so protective of her."

"Gross. I did *not* know that. Done. All interest lost."

Tundra flaps his wings and frowns at me. "Really? The fact that she is with child is the deterring factor?"

"Why wouldn't it be? I want no part of procreation. Who in their right mind would?"

We catch the updraft of a warm-air thermal and soar for a while without effort. Tundra tips right and body surfs the current of air staying over the trucks. "Just focus on Honor and only Honor or I'll kill you myself."

I roll my eyes. "That threat would hold more weight if you didn't say it to me every day."

Tundra grunts. "Yes, and I mean it every day."

Honor

Lounging in the back seat of one of the SUVs Hawk had brought through an expanded gate is the most normal I've felt in months. My time with Calli in the Human Realm was as real to me or more than this life. "It's like two worlds collide being here and riding in a truck like this. No conveyance AI. No auto-driving."

Lukas smiles and meets my gaze in the rear-view mirror. "No offense, but I'm happy to have my hands on the wheel and foot on the pedals. Call me old-fashioned but I like being in charge of the vehicle I'm in."

"You are old-fashioned," I say, chuckling.

Calli's reading something on the screen of her phone and laughs. "Lukas, open a nav channel and link us with Hawk's truck, they're laughing their asses off about something."

Lukas reaches up and opens a communications channel with the SUV at the front of this procession. The small screen on the dash flicks to life and we're looking at the interior of the first truck.

"Hey, Lukas."

"Hey. I heard from your little firebird that we're missing out on the joke. Does this have anything to do with the scene back at the castle?"

"Oh, yeah," Jaxx says, his Texan drawl thick and smooth. "Sorry, Honor, I messed with your generals. Those boys really don't have a sense of humor."

Calli starts chuckling and sends me an apologetic smile. "What did you do, puss?"

"I caught the falcon checkin' out your goods and put the fear of death into him. Brant backed me up and between the two of us we pretty much convinced the two of them that if they get caught oglin' you again, we'll fry them up and have them with gravy and biscuits."

I laugh. "No. I missed that. What did he do?"

Brant's deep bass laughter takes over. "I think it's safe to say that Dune's a breast man."

Calli looks down at her boobs and smiles. "Well, in all fairness, with the pregnancy, I've got lots to look at."

"Yes, you do, *Chigua*," Kotah says. "But the honor of admiring the girls is reserved and restricted to your fated mates."

Honor sighs and holds up her hands. "Hey, I only met them yesterday. I can't be held responsible."

Calli laughs. "I remember that feeling. It's crazy how quickly things change."

"I don't think much will change for your winter soldier,"

Brant says, laughing. "If Tundra gets wound up any tighter, that boy's gonna blow."

"Maybe he needs to unwind," Jaxx says. "When we get back, we should plan an extended family soiree."

Now Calli's laughing harder. "First off, Jaxx will make any situation an excuse to have a night of drinking. Second, you just scared the feathers off of those boys and played the tough and deadly card. Do you think they want to drink with you?"

Jaxx leans into the line of the camera and winks at us. "Oh, kitten, everybody wants to drink with me."

"Oh, we need Calli to wear something low cut and suggestive," Hawk says. "It'll be hilarious to see how that plays out."

Jaxx grins. "Why Mr. Barron, I like the way you think, mate."

I laugh. "Let's get through today first. If Rhylan and Lukas are right, we can expect—"

Tundra

The boom and hiss of weapon fire sounds off in the distance to our right and I catch the smoke trails of two launched hand-held rockets. "Incoming."

I dive toward the convoy. With the line of buildings on both sides and the way the sun is reflecting off the glass towers, there's no way the drivers see what's coming at them.

Dune and I are a hundred feet above them...

The rockets are three times that distance and closing in fast.

"Hard left," I shout, breaking from Dune and swooping down toward the king's truck. "Divert them."

I dive recklessly close to the royal convoy and skim the front hood. My sudden presence forces the dragon to alter its trajectory.

Dune does the same thing on the third truck, diverting Honor from the incoming artillery.

Unfortunately, our appearance has Rhylan and Lukas swerving through oncoming traffic. The detour is dangerous but spares them from the full impact.

The missiles strike.

The world around us detonates.

The explosion is tremendous. Conveyances are thrown like tumbleweeds. The ground heaves into the air and then rains down in chunks of rock and earth.

One of the missiles hits a small commuter conveyance that had the misfortune of swerving to miss the king's transport. The car explodes and the road bursts into a fiery war zone.

A tragedy.

Still, saving the royal couple must be the priority.

Saving the convoy from a direct hit didn't save them from serious damage.

Rhylan veers in front of a city bus but doesn't get clear of it. The back bumper is clipped and with the speed and weight of the bus, it sends the king's truck into a spin.

I watch in horror as the black vehicle glides sideways at an alarming speed until the tires hit the curb and the force of the collision lifts it off the ground.

It tumbles out of control.

Side, roof, side, wheels, side, roof.

When it finally comes to a halt, the mangled black box it's on its side, with the driver's side up.

As much as I want to check on Princess Honor, my first duty is to secure the Guardian of the Quadrant—that means King Creed.

Landing on top of the truck, I pull at the mangled side door.

Horns blare. Smoke rises. Oil burns.

I twitch my nose and try not to think about the likelihood this vehicle is about to catch fire and blow up.

There's a deep rumble of two very angry wildlings growling inside and then the dragon kicks his door. The flimsy metal shoots up beside me and hangs on mangled hinges over the side of the truck. "Slecking hell. What's with the dive bomb, asshole?"

"I diverted you from a direct hit from missile fire."

The dragon pulls himself free and scans the destruction of the road where they were only a moment ago. "Well, shit."

"That's one way to put it."

"Step back while I get this door open."

I do as I'm told as Rhylan launches into the air and explodes into his dragon form. Flapping his massive, leathery wings, he hovers over the passenger's door, drops down, and grips it with his mighty talons.

The door is no match for the dragon's might.

"Majesty," I say reaching into the mangled interior of the vehicle. "I need to secure you and your queen."

I give the man credit, even bleeding from his head and shaken, he doesn't hesitate. He reaches down to where Keyla is suspended in her seatbelt and brushes her hair back. "Keyla, wake up and look at me, Little Wolf. Are you all right?"

"Doc? You okay?" Rhylan says, back in his human form and reaching into the front seat of the truck.

"Other than being pissed and maybe a fractured rib or two—"

"Incoming," I point down the street, scanning the scene. "I've got five armed attackers coming from the street and another six out of buildings."

Rhylan finishes helping the bear out, while I pull King Creed free of the vehicle. The dragon unholsters his sidearm and hands it to the bear. "Cover us."

"Yep."

I guide the king to stand with his back against the truck,

placing myself between him and the foot soldiers bearing down on us. "Majesty, I need to evacuate you."

"Not happening, warrior," he snaps. "I'm not leaving without my queen. Rhy, get her out of there."

Rhylan is hanging inside the vehicle head first reaching to free Keyla from the wreck. "Little wolf? Sweetie, I need to get you and Creed out of here. Come on. Work with me."

"I'm trying," she grunts. "The way the truck collapsed, I'm stuck."

The king glares at the truck door. "Rhy, get her unstuck."

"I'm trying."

Scanning the rooftops, I check the lines of sight, very aware we are in the open and compromised with incoming hostiles. "Majesty. It's time. I must insist."

"He's right," Rhylan says, twisting to look at us. "Creed, go with Tundra. I can dragon roll the truck and Doc can get Keyla out."

"I'm not leaving her... you... any of you."

The long growl of Keyla's wolf rumbles in my chest. "Yes, you are. Two years without a Thornebane on the throne is too long. We've talked about this."

The dark-haired bear mate rounds the truck and meets the king's gaze. "We'll get her out—I swear—but right now, Dornte's future is more important."

Creed curses and scowls at me. "I hate this."

"No doubt, sire. Unfortunately, that changes nothing. Place your arms around my neck, majesty. I apologize, but I must pick you up." When he complies and I've got a solid hold on him, I push off the ground and fly him forward to the City Center.

The contingency if anything happens, is to get the royal couple to the fallback location where Rhylan and Lukas have backup teams at the ready.

That is where I go.

When I land in front of the recreational center on the city property, there seems to be a great deal of confusion. Several castle guards are out, staring at the smoke cloud darkening the horizon.

When they see I've brought the king, they rush out to surround us.

"Status One. Secure the king," I say, checking for any sign of danger in the area. The City Center is an open urban landscape with trees and statuary. I see no sign of advancing forces. "We have incoming hostiles in the corridor. Someone give me a shoulder blaster."

A senior officer rushes forward with four soldiers. He nods to one of the men to relinquish his weapon and I sling it over my shoulder.

"Where is the queen?" he asks.

"I'm going back for her now."

"Bring her to me, Tundra," the king says. "Please."

"What are my parameters, sire? Do you approve lethal force?"

The king looks up from being escorted toward safety. When my gaze locks with those ebony eyes, his cruel smile chills me to the marrow. "They tried to kill me and mine. Lethal force is most definitely approved."

"Understood."

I launch into the air and push to get back to the scene of devastation. Black smoke is billowing thick above the buildings, and it's clear more than one vehicle has caught fire.

I generally consider my flight time to be very fast but knowing the queen is in danger, and with the status of Lady Honor uncertain, every second is an eternity.

Lukas

Motherfucking hell. I push back from the airbag and press the button to release my seat belt. When nothing happens, I pull my utility knife from the thigh pocket of my fatigues and start sawing through the belt. "Honor? Calli? Are you ladies all right?"

"Yeah," Calli says. "If you consider being furious and peeing a little all right."

I slice through the tough nylon and free myself. "Pissed is perfect. That's where I am too. Are you sure you just peed a little and it's not fluids leaking from the baby due to the collision?"

"Nope. Just squirted. I should've gone before I left but with this little monster sitting on my bladder, it wouldn't have mattered."

Thank fuck. "Honor? How about you? You good?"

"Oh, yeah. I'm having a fucking party back here."

I shoulder my door open and fall out onto the street unsteady. Glaring up and down the burning roadway, I curse at the ten other cars that are in varying states of demolished and destroyed.

"Shadow? Are you all right?" When he doesn't answer, I round the front hood to the passenger's side and give his door a yank.

The elf is unconscious, and blood is smeared on the window and running down the right side of his face.

"Sorry for the aggressive detour, folks," Dune says, landing beside me. "We need to pack our bags and vacate as soon as possible."

"Shadow shouldn't be moved," Calli says. "He hit his head."

"Normally, I'd agree," Dune says, "but you're sitting ducks out here for another aerial attack."

"Aerial attack? Is that what happened?" Honor gets herself unbuckled and helps Calli get free. "One minute we're driving along, the next we're veering sideways into oncoming traffic."

"Sorry about that," Dune says, moving in beside me. "When the missiles were fired, I figured you'd rather crash than blow up."

Calli nods. "Good call, dude. Crash it is."

I build up a store of magic and melt the passenger's door lock with a bolt of energy. Once I get the door open, I frown at the smoke and chaos filling the war-torn street. "Let's figure out where the others are and where we're triaging. Shadow needs medical attention. Jaxx or Doc would be a big help."

Dune helps Honor and Calli out of the truck and scans the state of fire and rubble around us.

I give the counselor another visual check and curse.

He's got a nasty gash across his nose and is bleeding behind his ear from obvious head trauma. I free him from the wreck as quickly as I can and then glance up at the sound of running footsteps.

Pulling my gun, I support Shadow with one hand and am ready to fire with the other.

"Hold your fire," Hawk says, arriving with Jaxx.

Hawk closes in on Calli first and Jaxx's EMT first responder genes kick in and he comes to me.

"What are we looking at?" the jaguar asks.

"We swerved hard to miss Dune. He hit his head against the door."

"Has he been conscious at all?"

"No. Not yet."

Jaxx whistles between his teeth. "Falcon, can I get a hand with evac?"

Jaxx and Dune take over Shadow's situation and I jog over to check on the girls. "Ready to roll?"

Honor nods. "So much excitement for my first day back in the swing of things. Is this what I can expect?"

"Pretty much." I steady her footing, wishing she was stronger than she is.

Hawk's got one arm around Calli's back and the other hand on their baby. "Are you sure you're good, Spitfire? The seatbelt didn't cut into your belly?"

Calli shakes her head. "I'm one-hundy percent. Honest. Shadow is the only one who's hurt."

"Good. That's good," he says absently. "Well, not the part about Shadow being hurt, of course, but that you and little Liza are doing well."

Hawk and the others will lose their minds if something happens to their baby.

He meets my gaze and frowns. "Ready to roll out?"

I lift my gun, reach into the truck to pull a spare sidearm from the console for Honor, and scan the sheets of glass windows on the buildings above.

So far so good but our visibility is shit and once we leave the cover of crashed cars, we'll be in the open.

"Just another day at the office."

Dune and Jaxx get Shadow to his feet, and I search for a destination point. "Dune, did you see where Tundra took the others?"

"No. He diverted Creed's truck and I took Honor's."

Understandable. "See if you can locate them with an aerial sweep. Also, check for any incoming hostiles. Whoever hit us knew we'd be coming and chose this as their kill box. If they know what they're doing, they've got ground support moving in. Take out anyone who doesn't look friendly."

He frowns and looks to Honor. "Are those my orders, Princess?"

Honor nods. "Do as Lukas asks. Until we learn more about the state Dornte is in, it makes sense to let someone who knows better call the shots. While you do that, we'll take Shadow toward the other truck. If you can find out what happened to my brother, I'd appreciate it."

"Yes, Princess." Dune pushes off the ground and opens his

wings. I'm not a fan of the guy, but even still, I admit those wings are pretty fucking spank.

We get moving across the street and I brush a hand over my face. The stench of burnt rubber is singing my nostrils. It's nasty.

Honor is leaning on me more than I'd like. Not that I mind, I wish she felt stronger. I squeeze her wrist as we walk and flash her a smile. "Thank you, by the way."

"For what?" Honor asks.

"For backing me with your boy. I know protecting the crown gig is your territory but you're right. You three aren't up to speed yet. I'm not trying to step on anyone's toes—"

Tat-a-tat-tat.

The car window next to us explodes in a blast of glass shrapnel and I put my body between Honor and where the shots came from. As the next round of weapon fire comes in, Hawk and I tuck the girls behind two crashed cars and hunker down.

"Did anyone see who's firing at us?"

Cue the round of shaking heads.

All right. Plan B. "I'll try to find out—"

"No," Honor snaps as I move to leave. "You can't go out there. You're not bulletproof."

"*I* am." Calli pulls off her shoes and whips her dress off over her head. "One of you save my clothes. I'll need them later for the memorial."

"Calli, no," Hawk snaps.

"Yes," she says. "I'm safer as a phoenix and you know it. This human woman being fired at is the one who can get hurt."

I nod. "She's got a point."

"We don't know who we're dealing with," Hawk says. "I don't like it."

She points up as Tundra and Rhylan fly overhead. "I'll be in good company. You boys get Honor and Shadow to safety. I'll do what I do."

Hawk and Jaxx both curse.

I nod. "Yes ma'am."

CHAPTER TWELVE

Dune

𝓘 hate that human, but that doesn't mean I don't respect him. He's a quick thinker in the clutch and brave considering he has no physical assets like heightened senses or flight. He's somewhat competent as a soldier and a strategist. And damn it, by what I heard this morning, he's a decent lover too.

I still hate him.

It strikes me as the shooting starts that my duty as a General of the Crown is to protect King Creed and his wife and I don't know where they are. As I scan the wreckage of their truck, it's obvious they are long gone.

How am I supposed to earn respect as one of Princess Honor's warriors if I don't have a member of the crown to guard?

Another round of weapon's fire riddles the air and I dive and swoop out of the way. All right. If I can't protect the royal couple, I can at least stop the men who are actively trying to kill them.

I track where the shots are coming from.

Below me—that's obvious.

I climb a few dozen feet, leveling out at an altitude that keeps me beyond the range of blaster bolts.

"Where are they?" the massive dragon says, pulling up beside me.

"Down there somewhere."

"Not good enough, falcon," he snaps. "If someone has the balls to bomb my truck with me and my mates inside it, you've got to know what's going on. If that means you put yourself in the line of fire, you slecking well do it."

"Where are the king and queen?"

"Tundra took Creed to the City Center. Doc, Kotah, and Brant took Keyla into one of the buildings to start triaging the citizens."

"And Honor?"

"No idea. Focus on what's in front of us and we can have a reunion later." He drops in a *whoosh* of his mighty wings and starts searching the urban setting.

The shooting restarts almost immediately.

"Got them… behind those bronze sculptures. Two men in street bandit rags… and four more on the opposite side of the road trying to circle them."

The scorching heat of the phoenix announces the arrival of Calli before we see or hear her. "I'll get those six. You boys find me some more to fry."

Tundra flies overhead. "Where is the queen?"

"I don't know. The king's truck is overturned and empty." I go back to scanning the war-torn street below.

"Find Queen Keyla and secure her," Tundra says. "I'll help Calli and Rhylan secure the street."

"One problem with that plan," I say. "I don't know where they are. How about *you* secure the queen and *I* help with the fight?"

He looks at me and frowns. "You need to take this seriously, Dune. Lives are at stake."

I roll my eyes. "Just go. You can belittle me later."

For once, Tundra lets me win an argument. Will wonders never cease. I watch his white feathers cut through the morning sky and shake myself.

He's trusting me to do my job?

Then I guess I better do my job.

Getting my head back into the fight, I laugh at the battle in progress. Calli's massive firebird is breathing long streams of fire and frying the rebel bandits like bacon sizzling on a skillet.

She's already taken care of the six I pointed out, so I'm up to find her a few more.

"I'll fly down and get a better look. Maybe I can even draw fire and flush a few more out."

Wait. Did I just volunteer to be the bait?

Where did that come from?

Too late now.

Tipping forward, I flap my wings for a couple of strong strokes and then tuck them back and let gravity and aerodynamics take hold.

As I plummet toward the street, I scan the storefront stoops, apartment vestibules, and places where people might hide. "I've got three bandits rounding the corner by the overturned SUV."

I don't know if the men I've spotted hear me or sense me or simply pick that moment to turn around and find me bearing down on them but in the turning of the tides, now I'm the one being spotted and targeted.

I stiffen and activate my armor. Invisible to the eyes of men, a layer of impermeable membrane covers the wings of the Elbirfae and when we activate our protection, it hardens to near steel.

That doesn't mean getting shot doesn't sting.

It does.

It hurts as bad as having tape ripped off your scrotum. Seriously. I've had that happen and it hurts.

But even that is better than energy bolts and bullets penetrating flesh and ripping you open.

My downward momentum is so great that when I get to the spot where the street rats are firing at me, I simply open my wings, pivot so I'm moving feet first, and hit the closest one with my steel-toed boots.

The impact knocks the first one flying back.

I take advantage of their shock to rip the throats open of the other two with my talons. Tossing them out onto the street, Calli makes sure they're good and dead by burning the bodies.

"That one's mine," Rhylan says, landing on the sidewalk as a man. "I need one to question. Sadly, we can't kill them all." He grips the punk with the face paint by the collar and grins. "Congratulations, asshole. You get to be the one who lives."

"Fuck you. I won't spill anything you piece of shit."

"Two more over here," Calli calls.

"Cool, save me one. This one says he won't talk." He lets go of the guy and turns to me. "He's of no use to me. Go ahead and kill him."

The guy looks from me to the men on the ground with their throats ripped out. "What? Whoa... wait... Fine, I'll talk! I'll talk!"

Rhylan turns back. "You better not think you're playing me 'cause I will end you the second you start to stall out."

The guy shakes his head so hard he's likely scrambling his gray matter. "I'm not playing you. Seriously. I'm your guy."

The dragon shrugs. "Fine, I'll take him back to the castle and lock him down. Dune, you watch Calli and get her back to her mates. Then, if you see my mates, tell them I'll be back."

I nod. "Got it."

I jog out to the street carnage and assess what's happening

with the phoenix. She's the real deal and damn, she's bigger and scarier than I thought she'd be.

And she seems to enjoy torching people.

When she finishes with that group of rebels, she looks down at me. "Who's next?"

"I don't see any more."

"Where did the missiles come from?"

I point in the direction of the three silver high-rises off to our left and up the street. "I'm sure the shooters are long gone by now."

"Agreed, but there's no sense being lazy. We might as well check it out. You game for a leisurely tour around the sky?"

I open my wings and launch into the air. "Yeah, I guess so. I could stretch my wings."

~

Honor

Lukas, Hawk, and Jaxx get Shadow and me across the street and around the wreckage of the other SUV without much of an issue. Calli, Dune, and the dragon twin are focused on taking care of the men shooting at us. Calli seems to be enjoying herself.

"I can't believe that's my Calli girl. It's crazy how much has changed."

Lukas catches me watching my best friend blazing as a fiery bird against the morning sky. "She's something to behold, that's for sure."

"And much more impressive now that she doesn't face plant in the dirt every time she flies," Jaxx adds.

"I kinda miss picking sticks out of her hair," Hawk says, checking his watch. He looks up and points to one of the buildings with a restaurant off to our right. "They're in here."

"How do you know?" I ask.

"Because we've been doing this a long time and have an intricate tracking system built into our watches."

We make our way toward the restaurant Hawk pointed out, skirting the building and cutting off any line of sight as closely as we can.

We've got a good pace going until Shadow groans and starts to convulse.

Jaxx curses, setting him down on the sidewalk as quickly and gently as he can. "Shit. We'll need a minute here, folks."

Lukas drags a public garbage bin along the sidewalk and tucks behind it. "It's not great cover. As soon as he can move, Jaguar. You let us know."

Hawk's focus glasses over and then he nods. "Brant is coming. He'll help with cover."

Lukas nods and hands me his gun. "When Brant gives us our window, I'll help Jaxx with Shadow. You and Hawk focus on keeping us from getting sniped."

I grip his gun and nod. "I can shoot, by the way. If you were wondering."

He flashes me a sexy smile. "You're the Guardian of the Crown. I never doubted that for a second."

There's not an ounce of teasing in his husky words and how sexy is that?

The four of us crouch at the ready until things seem to settle for Shadow. Jaxx lets off a long sigh and nods at Hawk. "Okay, tell them we're set to move."

Hawk gets that spacey look in his eyes again and then Brant and Dillan rush out carrying steel tables like two juggernauts with metal umbrellas.

"Good to see you all upright and breathing," Brant says, holding his table up to shield us.

"You too," Lukas says. "Doc, the elf needs an appointment for a look-see ASAP. He hit his head on the car window during the accident. He hasn't regained consciousness and he just had a seizure."

The bear wildling hands his table to Hawk and kneels to assist Jaxx. "I don't suppose we have a backboard or a collar handy."

"Not on me, no."

"All right take the legs off one of the tables and we'll lay him out and get him inside with as much support to his neck and head as we can."

Hawk is about to set his table down when Brant grips the steel pedestal leg coming out the bottom of his table and snaps it off like a twig. He hands it to Jaxx and then takes Hawk's table to continue giving us cover.

Jaxx and Doc get Shadow laid out and then the two of them walk off carrying their makeshift backboard with Brant shielding them every step.

"Shit. Just how strong is that guy?" I ask watching him trot off.

"Brant?" Lukas follows my gaze. "I wouldn't even hazard a guess to what he could lift. He's a beast, that's for sure. He and the dragon seem to be on a par."

"Holy shit."

"Let's get inside." Hawk gestures for Lukas and me to head toward the door to the restaurant. A couple of shots follow our path, but nothing hits close enough to be alarmed about.

The air is chilled inside and my heated skin cools fast and gives me goosebumps. I take in the scene and frown at all the injured citizens.

It's not only our group that has gathered in here but dozens of people from the street are taking refuge too.

The tables have been cleared to the side and people in varying degrees of broken and bleeding are reclining in booths, on the ground, and in chairs—a pop-up clinic aiding citizens and friends.

Keyla is bandaging a mother of two and making the kids laugh. When she sees Shadow, she excuses herself and rushes to check on him.

"She's got a nurturing side. I'll give her that."

Lukas arches a brow. "She's hands down one of the most loving and empathetic people I've ever met... except maybe tied with her brother."

I shrug. "Dornte needs more than a kiss on the forehead and a bandage over our boo-boo. We're in a battle for the crown here. We need a warrior queen, not a nursemaid."

Lukas chuckles but there's no humor in the sound. "Then keep watching. Your past few years made you cynical. You're judging Keyla on things you know nothing about."

When my brother's little wolf finishes speaking with Doc and Jaxx, she jogs over to check on us. "Are you both all right? Do you need water or medical care?"

I wave away her concern. "Where's my brother?"

"Tundra evacuated him first thing."

I draw a deep breath more than a little relieved. "I'm surprised Creed agreed to that."

Rhylan comes in and kisses Keyla's cheek. "It was very much against his will. Keyla was trapped in the truck for a bit, and he wanted to stay and help."

Keyla frowns at the gash on Rhylan's jaw. "Your brother found himself aggressively outvoted."

"Three to one," Rhylan says, winking at her. "Majority rules."

Keyla nods. "Yes, it does."

What a dumbass. "His priority has to be to the citizens of Dornte. He can't storm into situations and put himself at risk."

Brant chuckles. "Tell that to the mighty dragons of Travon. You should've seen what we did to their super-secret dragon lair when they captured Rhylan and tried to execute him for falling in love with Creed."

"Good times," Jaxx says, glancing up from helping Doc care

for Shadow. "We trashed that place real good and showed them who's king."

"Fucking right we did," Brant says.

"Hey, I'm heading out to find our girl," Hawk says, checking the magazine of his gun. "Anyone want to come play find the fiery mate with me?"

Kotah and Brant raise their hands and move toward the door.

"Bring her home, boys," Jaxx says, holding Shadow's head straight as Doc evaluates him.

I remember the bundle of fabric tied around my waist and jog to catch up with them as they exit. "Here, Calli asked us to save her clothes so she'd be presentable for the memorial. Not that we're in any condition to go."

Keyla frowns. "It doesn't matter what we're wearing or how sooty or scraped up we are, we're going to that memorial. To miss it strikes a win for the rebels."

"Fuck the rebels," Doc says, kneeling close by. "Oh, sorry, was that my outdoor voice?"

Keyla offers him a warm smile. "You can use any voice you want, Bear. You're rocking this crisis."

When Hawk, Brant, and Kotah exit the restaurant, I stare out at the street and the damage is hard to reconcile. Less than an hour ago, these people were safe and whole and going about their daily lives.

Now their lives might never be the same.

"Can I get some help here?" A man calls out from a side door leading to the street.

"Yep." Lukas holsters his gun and leads the way.

I follow, tight to his very fine ass. The man is intense and impressive when pouring a cup of coffee in the kitchen. When hostiles are moving in and he's on high alert, he's downright breathtaking.

Keyla grabs a first aid kit on the run and follows without hesitation.

The man who called us holds the door open until the three of us exit. That's when I catch the intentions of his mental energy. I turn to study whether it's just the chaos of the attack that's affecting him or if he's—

He whistles and the *bang* of the metal door slamming behind us signals our retreat being cut off.

"Take her out, boys."

A dozen street bandit skinheads ooze out of the shadows and stoops. The three of us tighten our ranks as the cobblestone seating area fills with armed bandits.

Lukas curses, throwing up an iridescent shield in front of us, but there are six others behind us and closing in hard and fast.

The man's words strike me cold. *Take her out.*

Personal feelings about Keyla aside, there's no way the Queen of Dornte is getting assassinated on my first day as the Guardian of the Crown.

I lift my weapon to defend her, but she's already shifted into a stunning white wolf and is launching through the air with her canines bared.

Lukas squeezes off a few rounds and then the restaurant's outer patio explodes into a battlefield.

Our ambushers have the advantage of cover except for the one who lured us out here.

Keyla has gripped his wrist in her maw and her teeth have sunk deep. Despite his screams in protest, she's shaking her head, tearing his flesh like a beast.

Unable to use his gun, he's defenseless against Lukas's bullets. Two shots to the chest and he drops.

Keyla releases him and turns her head to assess the next opponent. With her teeth bared and blood staining her pristine coat, I'm suddenly not seeing the child bride anymore.

Without hesitating, the two of them move to the next man who comes at her.

Shit. They have obviously fought together before because they have a rhythm. I don't have that advantage.

Not with him or any of them.

I push down the anger that fires inside me and focus on doing my duty.

When a loading bay door opens and another two dozen armed assailants ooze out onto the street, the three of us curse and stop fighting.

"Run!"

CHAPTER THIRTEEN

Tundra

The sound of weapons discharging draws me away from the main intersection where the most severe damage has been sustained and over one block to where a wave of weaponized punks are closing in on Lukas, Honor, and the queen in her white wolf form.

They are overwhelmingly outnumbered and retreating with as much speed as they can harness.

I tilt my shoulders forward and dive to intercept their fight. With my natural shielding engaged on my wings, a great deal of my body becomes impenetrable.

Sadly, it doesn't protect my limbs or my core.

If I'm shot in the chest. I'll end up as dead as the men Lukas is dropping in the street.

By telegraphing their escape route, I catch up and land as they bank a corner. Lukas senses my arrival and spins. He's fast with his gun but doesn't fire.

Speaking in tongues, he swipes his hand through the air, and magic tingles over my skin. He's not looking at me though, his sights are set on the air behind me. "That will hold them back for a moment."

When the firing continues, I spread out my wings and block everything coming at us from behind just in case. "Queen Keyla. Allow me to take you to Creed."

The white wolf turns around and runs back as Lukas and Honor stand behind the screen of my plumage and catch their breath.

Rushing back, she transforms with a grace I can't help but admire. One moment she's on four legs as a fierce white wolf and the next she's morphing into an equally stunning young queen. "I can't leave—"

"Tundra is right," Lukas says. "Honor and I will be fine. In fact, we'll take the visual screening Tundra is offering and I'll work some magic. Get somewhere safe."

I nod. "I shall escort her to the City Center fallback recreation building as planned."

Lukas holds out his hand to Honor. "Good enough. We'll meet you there."

"No," the queen argues. "Four is better than two."

I grunt. "The sting of metal is a sign that Lukas's spell is failing. I'm afraid I must insist, Majesty."

Keyla frowns and turns to face the human. "Promise me you have a plan, Lukas."

He winks and pulls Honor into a recessed doorway. When he raises his hands, they disappear, the brick of the exterior wall extending across in front of them, concealing them from sight.

Keyla seems satisfied they will be all right and steps in close to my chest.

"Place your arms around my neck and hold tight. I am sorry, but I must invade your space and hold onto you as well."

She chuckles, smiling up at me. "Tundra. You're being shot from behind and rescuing me from attackers. Holding me to ensure I don't fall is hardly offensive."

When she's ready, I scoop under her knees, lift her against my chest, and launch into the air.

As much as I want to help Honor, as an Amberloq General, my duty is to secure the crown.

I do, however, take comfort in the knowledge that Lukas is with our princess. As unexpected as he is as an addition to our force, he is an asset.

"Look at the devastation," Keyla says, frowning down at the streets below. "Such a tragedy."

I scan the smoldering rubble and couldn't agree more. "This madness must end. These people who believe themselves justified to torment the lives of our citizens for the sake of money and power need to be stopped."

"They will be. I give you my word."

We fly in silence for a time and then I slow to land in the exact spot I left the king twenty minutes earlier. "Come, Majesty. I'm sure the king will be anxious to—"

"Thank the Powers." Creed rushes out of the turnstile door of the building with a stream of worried-looking guards racing to keep up.

I step back to give them a moment as the king kisses her as passionately as if the two of them were in the privacy of their home.

No one seems to mind.

When he steps back, Creed looks at me. "Thank you, Tundra. What is our status? Is everyone all right?"

"There are still bandits in the streets, so I must return quickly. As far as I know, Shadow is the only one from the castle group who is truly hurt."

"I'm sorry to hear that. Yes, please go be of aid. We'll be here. And thank you, Tundra. You've done well today. I'm thankful you and Dune are here to help."

I dip my chin and then push off and head back to find Honor and Dune.

∼

Lukas

Honor Thornebane blows my mind. Two days out of a catatonic state and she's running the streets and fighting off attackers, and despite feeling underprepared and weak from her incarceration, she got off a few impressive shots and is giving it her all.

Now, enclosed in a three-foot square space, I have shut out the world and there is nothing but her and me... and my rapid pulse rate... and the sweat glistening on her exposed skin... and the adrenaline hard on I always get when fighting through a dangerous situation.

"I should warn you," I whisper into the shell of her ear. "I find a fierce woman very sexy. There is no more potent an aphrodisiac for me, especially after a firefight when adrenaline is pumping."

Her throaty chuckle is sexy... but not nearly as sexy as the way she wriggles her ass back against my stiff cock. "And here we are, stuck all alone in this confining space until the coast is clear."

"Here we are."

"How long will this glamor spell hold and keep us hidden from the prying eyes of all those men?"

"The spell isn't the issue. It's whether or not they have someone sensitive to magic in their crew."

She turns to our right and frowns at the metal door that leads into the building. "Then I guess we should make tracks and get some distance from the bad guys."

"That would be one option, yes." I wait a beat to see how she wants to play this and when she doesn't move, I'm stuck between berating myself for being an idiot and sending up a prayer of thanks.

But really, we don't know what's behind that door.

It might be safer to remain isolated from the world.

She turns to face me, and a ripple of electrical charge sweeps over my skin, heightening my sensations. Abruptly, the danger is closer, the space we're in tighter, and the sensuality of having her here wanting me more arousing.

I'm hungry for her, my mouth watering as I slide my hands over the navy bodice of her outfit to cup her heaving breasts. "What does it mean to your Amberloq men if we continue to explore what's building between us?"

"That's my call, not theirs. The way the joining of the generals works is that they follow my lead."

"And what does it mean for you and me?"

She shrugs. "Do you need to define it?"

"No. I'm simply gauging where we are."

She runs her palms up my chest and stops to thumb my nipples hidden beneath my shirt. "I want you. Right now, it's a no strings, no expectation thing for me. Is that all right?"

I swallow, her little thumb massage making my already hard cock pulse in anticipation. "I can live in the moment, sure. I'm not supposed to be complicating your life, remember?"

She grins. "I think orgasms *uncomplicate* things. They make it easier to make it through the miasma of a chaotic day."

"That's deep."

"Speaking of deep... if you don't mind granting me another favor... I have this ache..."

I chuckle and cup the back of her neck pulling her closer. "Let me help you with that."

Our bodies crash together, her arms encircling my ribs as my hands grip her hair and wrap her braid around my fist like a satin rope. With a tug, I pull her head to the side, baring the smooth column of her throat to me.

I drop my mouth and nip at her tender flesh before working my way up her jaw to claim her kiss.

She groans, her purple eyes glittering with magic as her

tongue invades my mouth in deep plunges. The ferocity of her passion unlocks something primal in me and I pull back to breathe before I pass out.

"You should know... we're safe. I'm clean and get the male injection to stop pregnancy."

"Stop talking."

I chuckle. "My princess is hot and bothered."

Pinning her against the brick, I reach under her split skirt and find the hook and zipper to her slacks on her hip. The fine silver fabric falls to her ankles, leaving those long legs bare to me.

I slide my fingers beneath the soft silk of her panties and delve into the heat pooled between her legs.

She gasps.

"So hungry."

"I've been a captive for years, in a coma for months, and we were almost killed today. I want to feel alive and in control of my life."

"You're alive, Princess... and so fucking hot."

She unbuckles my waistband and shoves my pants and boxers down my thighs. Reaching under my shirt, she pulls me forward to pin her against the brick with erotic abandon.

"Please," she gasps against my lips. "I need this."

My cock is thick and hard, bobbing anxiously to get inside her. I grip the fleshy rounds of her ass and lift her off her feet, pressing her against the wall at her back. There's no need to guide my erection, it knows exactly where it needs to be and finds the heat of her core without hesitation.

Thrusting forward, I close my eyes and let the glide and slide of her greedy muscles milk my cock.

She claims my mouth in a rough, lust-fueled kiss, gripping my shoulders with bruising force as I pick up a rhythm. Adrenaline has keyed us both up.

Closing my eyes, I let the sensations wash over me.

The warm suction of in and out. The pinching grip of her nails against my shoulder. Our breathy pants building as my thighs flex and my hips rock.

I glance to my left to check that my glamor is holding and my privacy spell is containing the slap of flesh and her feminine sounds.

She's not going to last.

Her body is tightening around me and I place a gentle hand over her mouth to catch her throaty cries.

Her release hits in a wild rush, her pussy clutching and squeezing me. I clench my jaw, riding out her ecstasy as I return my hold to her ass and my own orgasm bears down on me.

Fuck she feels good.

When her orgasm fades, my hammering thrusts quicken. It doesn't take long before ragged breath tears from my chest as I stiffen. Throwing my head back, I pant through the constriction of my abs and the release of cum in pulsing, streams inside her.

My thigh muscles quiver under the strain of the position but it's still a fucking shame to pull out.

"At another time, in another place, I'd go longer. Sadly, we're still in a compromised location and everyone will be wondering and worrying about us."

And the fucking quint will smell the sex.

I roll my eyes, not looking forward to the smirks and comments about to bite me in the ass.

Too bad. This was so worth the ribbing.

With my breathing still heavy, I kiss the bare skin of Honor's collarbone and ease out of her. The loss of heat is a hardship. "Promise me we'll do this again soon and spend the time to get it right."

She casts me a warm smile, her purple eyes dancing. "Oh, yeah. I want to orgasm around you again as soon as possible, and ride your cock, and feel this alive again and again and again."

I reach down and pull her panties back into place. "Imagine me cleaning you properly and treating you with the respect you deserve. The first opportunity we get, we do this again I'll give you the royal treatment."

"With many orgasms," she says.

I chuckle and lean forward to brush a kiss over her lips. "Yes, many orgasms. Many, many orgasms."

And just like that, my cock is hardening again.

Dune

After the streets quiet down and Rhylan returns from dumping his prisoner back at the castle, he brings a cleanup crew, and they take over the mayhem.

That leaves me free to figure out our next steps.

The only one of Hawk's trucks that survived the missile attack is being used to transport Shadow back to the castle medical center so that leaves the majority of the royal family and friends with no way to get to the memorial celebration.

Until I come up with a brilliant plan.

Returning to the restaurant where Doc and the phoenix quint are treating the injured, I gesture toward the door grinning from ear to ear. "All aboard, folks. I've commandeered us a city bus. Next stop, the Dornte War Memorial celebration of life."

Tundra frowns. "And when you say commandeered, do you mean you're stealing the bus that crashed into the royal transport?"

I grin. "Maybe. The point is, it's here, we're here, there are enough seats for everyone, and it's already off-schedule so there's no reason not to use it."

Tundra doesn't seem to share my logic. "We're waiting on

Princess Honor and Lukas. I thought they'd have been here by now, but—"

"We're here," Honor says, raising a hand as she and the human arrive. "We got pinned but Lukas magicked us up an escape and we waited things out."

"Pinned, eh?" Hawk says, grinning at Lukas. "That must've been terrible for you both. Glad to see you weathered the storm and came out unscathed."

I'm pretty sure I'm missing something because the wildlings are all fighting back smirks.

Whatever. Fae from the Human Realm are odd.

"Does anyone want to continue to the ceremony?"

Honor nods, her cheeks unusually flushed. "Absolutely, let's load up and head out."

It takes us longer to get the bus around the debris littering the streets than it does to get to the Dornte City Center where the memorial has been constructed.

I'm not sure if the news of the attack downtown has brought people out of their homes, but the event is even more heavily attended than we were told to expect.

When I pull the city bus to a stop at the curb, I grip the handle and swing the doors open. "This stop, the Thornebane celebration of life. Everybody out."

Our arrival draws the attention of the crowd but there seems to be even more interest when Keyla and Creed exit the recreation center to meet us.

There's a momentary buzz of shock while people try to figure out what happened and why the king and queen are coming out of the building covered in grease and soot and why the rest of us were riding on a broken and battered bus.

Creed strides straight toward the podium and after a brief moment whispering with the event coordinator, is introduced to a roaring round of applause.

"Blessed be. Thank you all, so much for coming. I'm sorry we look like we were dragged out of a burning war zone but that's exactly what happened."

There's a general look of horror over the crowd and he holds up his hands. "The fates were with us today, but due to a rebel attack assisted by rogue street bandits, a section of the downtown corridor is now badly in need of restoration."

Creed gives the attendees a moment to absorb the news and many of them turn to view the smokey skies in the distance.

"Was anyone killed?" Someone shouts.

"Hawk's new trucks suffered a brutal death," Brant rumbles so only we can hear him.

"Not important," Hawk says. "Loss of life is far more important. I'm just thankful our mates and family aren't among today's dead."

"Amen, to that, hotness," Calli says, resting her head against her mate's chest.

Hawk's arm comes around her and his hand rests against her belly. Yeah, there it is. And baby makes six.

Pushing that out of my mind, I return my attention to Creed's address.

"Yes, there were casualties. Keyla and I have a dear friend who was badly injured, as well as countless others who were hurt as well as killed. Please keep our citizens in your thoughts and prayers in the days ahead and know we grieve with you."

"Will it ever end?" Someone asks.

Creed draws a deep breath and exhales. "As much as I would love to say the civil unrest and criminal behavior Laryssa incited is gone, there are still those who cling to her methods of quadrant management. Violence. Intimidation. And fearmongering."

Keyla reaches for his hand, and he winks at his mate before continuing. "Be patient. Be vigilant. And know your queen and I, with the help of Princess Honor and the Amberloq, and the

Phoenix Quint, will right the wrongs of the past and ensure a brighter future."

Honor steps up beside him and the two of them present a united front. "Look forward to new beginnings," Honor says. "And on that note, I'd like to say a few words about our parents and the hopes they held for this quadrant."

CHAPTER FOURTEEN

Honor

By the time we get back to Thornebane Castle, everyone is tired, hungry, and we're still covered in the remnants of violence. The three camps decide to take a break for a bite to eat, wash up, and have a nap.

None of us are ready for one of Jaxx's social events with Shadow still in serious condition. And even if everyone was well, after hearing the tales of shenanigans they get up to while drunk and disorderly, I'm not sure I'll ever be ready for a Jaxx event.

The four of us return to the suite and Lukas sets his hand against the scanner to let us in.

"Tomorrow," I grouse. "Tomorrow we reprogram the scanner to recognize me and let me enter my own apartment."

"It's a date," Lukas says, winking at me.

"You are in for a treat, Princess," Dune says, holding up two big bags of takeout food. "Mareegan's has the best food this side of the desert."

Lukas chuckles. "I'm not sure if that's a selling point or not, my feathered friend."

Dune's gaze narrows. "It is."

"In two years, things could've changed," Tundra says.

"No. Some things never change. Mareegan's greatness is one of them. Now, where are the plates?"

Lukas tilts his head toward the hallway that leads to the kitchen and Dune falls in behind him. When he's halfway down the hall, he looks back. "Aren't you coming, Princess?"

I hold up my hand. "Give me two minutes to take off these clothes and get changed. I smell like a junkyard gone bad and it's souring my appetite."

Tundra chuckles. "Nothing sours Dune's appetite."

The falcon frowns. "If you were raised on desert vermin and rotisserie lizards, you'd celebrate food too."

I chuckle as he and Lukas head into the kitchen and then hold up a hand toward Tundra. "Do you mind?"

"Not at all, Princess." He steadies my balance while I take off my shoes.

When that's taken care of, I lift my hair. "Would you mind unzipping the back of my dress?"

"Not at all, Princess."

I chuckle and swing around to smile at him. "Please call me Honor. If we are to become... whatever we're to become, you have to stop being so formal with me."

"As you wish."

When the fastening of my bodice is unzipped, I thank him, shuffle to my room to get changed, and close the door behind me.

Only... I don't get changed.

Plunking down on the edge of the bed I draw a deep breath and try to sort out the jumble of emotions swirling in my head like a twister....

This is my life now.

The conflict in the realm isn't going away anytime soon. There will be more battles. There will be more death. And when things like this happen, it'll be me the quadrant looks to for answers.

I need to restore my strength.

I need to get caught up on the players against us.

I need an army to help me keep the citizens safe.

Letting the reality of all that take root, my thoughts drift to what went wrong today. Too much. It might just be easier to try to figure out what went right...

"Knock-knock," Lukas says on the other side of the door. "You good?"

"Yeah, come in."

He opens the door and slides his head and shoulders in the crack, offering me an apologetic smile. "Sorry to disturb you. We thought you might have fallen asleep or something."

I straighten and frown at the purple swelling rising to the surface of his left cheekbone. I suppose we can all expect some bruising over the next few days.

"Honor? Is everything all right?"

"Sure, why wouldn't it be?"

"You've been in here almost forty-five minutes."

"I have? Oh, sorry. I guess I got thinking about things. Today was intense."

"It was. Do you want to talk about it?"

I stand, pull my bodice and skirt over my head, and step into my closet. Unzipping my slacks, I let them fall to the plush, beige carpet.

I step into a pair of cotton pants and pull a stretch knit over my head before heading back out. "It's ironic. Shadow told me to call on him if I ever needed to talk and now I do and he's hurt. Have we heard anything about his recovery yet?"

Lukas nods. "We all carry a vial of phoenix tears with us for emergencies. I managed to get some in him when I first pulled him from the truck. Doc sent word that he seems to be responding. For the moment, he's resting. If elves heal the same way we do, he'll wake up tomorrow with one hell of a headache, but he'll be fine."

"That's good. I forgot about the whole healing powers of phoenix tears thing."

Lukas comes fully into my bedroom and closes the door behind him. Wow, that bruise on his cheek looks painful. "Those tears have come in handy many times over the past six months."

As he comes deeper into the room, he's followed by Dune and then Tundra looking frustrated. "Excuse the intrusion, Princess. It seems Dune's desire to check on you negated his sense of privacy."

Dune frowns and gives Tundra the finger. "Lukas came in and he's not even one of her generals."

There's no missing the animosity there.

There's also no missing that Dune's lip is swelling and there's fresh blood trickling from his nose. I jog into the bathroom and return with a box of tissues, handing them to Dune before my carpet suffers yet another stain.

Having all three of them in here at once threatens to choke the air with testosterone and aggression, but hey, that's been the theme of the day.

Lukas leans back against the edge of my dresser and offers me a stoic smile. "What kept your wheels spinning for the better part of the past hour?"

Dune snorts. "Other than a rebel attack and being in a car wreck and Shadow getting hurt and standing through a memorial dedicated to your parents and thousands of other dead citizens."

I chuckle. "Really? Is this how things are now?"

"Is what how things are?" Dune asks.

I draw a deep breath and exhale. "It sickens me that Creed

was almost killed today. It was my first event in the first week of being the Guardian of the Crown and everything was almost lost."

"But it wasn't," Lukas says. "We pulled it together. And all's well that ends as well as can be expected."

Dune frowns. "I'm not an expert on Human Realm sayings, but I don't think that's how it goes."

I chuckle. "No. He was amending it for my benefit."

Dune nods. "Well, I think it was ironic that we pushed through the violence of attack to celebrate at the memorial. In my opinion, it strengthened the message to the citizens that we are resilient and won't ever stop fighting the chaotic forces."

Tundra arches an ebony brow. "That was both poignant and insightful, Dune. I'm impressed."

My desert general straightens. "I come up with a good one now and then."

Lukas moves to sit on the bed next to me and squeezes my knee. "And he's right. Like you said, this was your first event in your first week as Guardian of the Crown. Yes, there is room to improve, but when I first started whipping the quint into shape, they were much worse. Calli wanted nothing to do with her destiny and the guys were at each other's throats. You'll get this."

I take a deep breath and nod. "I know we will. Okay, let's eat. My stomach is cannibalizing itself and I'm dying to try food that is the best this side of the desert."

Lukas squeezes my hand and kisses the top of my head when he stands. "Perfect. We managed to hold Dune off to wait for you."

Dune grunts. "Sorry, but if you'd taken another ten minutes, all bets were off."

Tundra pushes Dune towards the door and our falcon's feathers ruffle. "We will always wait for you, Princess. Even if I have to tie Dune up and sit on him to ensure it."

I laugh, accepting Lukas's outstretched hand to pull me off to my feet. "Hopefully, it won't come to that."

Lukas

The four of us share a meal together and despite Dune being an egocentric dick and us coming to blows while waiting for Honor to change, he is right about the food. I've never tasted nomadic cuisine but it is very good.

Once we're finished eating, I call Doc and check in on Shadow and give everyone the confirmation. "He is indeed out of danger and resting. He was released from the castle medical center and is in the spare room of the King's Tower. Doc and Keyla are tending to him."

"That is good news," Tundra says.

"It is."

Honor is still anxious though and I'm not sure how to settle her down. She wants to feel like she's making headway as the Guardian of the Crown. I understand the impulse but she's not strong enough to work out and train physically more than once a day.

The raid was quite enough.

Mentally, she's struggling to find purchase as well.

"Tell me about the Amberloq," I say, trying to find a subject that won't directly reflect on her. "You mentioned yesterday it was primarily made up of Elbirfae in the past. Where did they live? How did they train? Why focus so heavily on Elbirfae?"

"Because we're slecking awesome," Dune snaps.

Tundra rolls his eyes. "Our natural tendency to be warriors coupled with the fact that we fly and can activate the shielding on our wings to become almost impenetrable to weapon's fire made us ideal candidates to defend the throne. It's a long-standing symbiosis between our race and the quadrant of Dornte."

"And where did your army live prior to the raids?"

Honor breaks the desert biscuit that came with our dinner and pops it in her mouth. "Amberloq Hall is where they were supposed to live but when Valorous and my father had their falling out, she moved the army off the castle grounds. I'm not sure how she had things set up or where. She was supposed to be my mentor, but she didn't come around much."

"Where is Amberloq Hall?"

She stretches her legs and walks to the balcony door, waving for me to follow. "Do you see that bronze peak beyond the line of trees? That's the roof of the crow's nest at the top of the attic."

Tundra looks at me with a question in his eyes.

I nod. "Oh, yeah, I definitely think so."

Honor frowns and looks at me. "What did I miss?"

"An expedition," Tundra says, standing. "Could we explore the old facility and see how things fared?"

Honor frowns out at the landscape and shrugs. "It's been boarded up and forgotten for close to twenty years. Creed and I made it our playhouse as kids but even we haven't been there for over a decade."

"Then I think a road trip is definitely in order," Lukas says. "In fact, I say we go right now."

"Now?" Honor says, her eyebrow arching sharply. "It's almost nightfall and we've been on the go all day."

I shrug. "If you don't want to—"

"No, I'm not saying that."

"Excellent, then let's go exploring."

Dune grins. "I'll pack food and drinks."

"And I'll pack a box of cleaning supplies and light bulbs," Tundra says.

I strike off and head for my room. "Excellent. I'll grab my duffle of tools and flashlights."

Honor shrugs. "Okay, I'm up for an adventure."

Tundra

Lukas may be a tough military man and a lethal opponent, but he has a definite soft spot for Honor. He and I are alike in that regard.

His idea about uncovering the Amberloq history and how they fit—or didn't—with the quadrant in the last reign works to bring Honor out of her frustration and give us all an actionable goal to focus on.

Which is good.

Less chance that Dune will spout off and start a fistfight in the kitchen.

"These grounds are more expansive than they seem," Lukas says, as we hike through the forested area between Thornebane Castle and Amberloq Hall. "I know Keyla and Kotah go out for a run every morning and evening when he's here, but I didn't realize they had so much land to explore."

Honor's appraising gaze takes in the trees and manicured pathways with a private smile. "My mother used to insist Creed and I spend a few hours out here playing every day. I think she saw how my father's relationship deteriorated with his sister and tried to give us a solid foundation of friendship."

"It seems to have worked," I say, reaching to pull back an overgrown branch hanging low into the path. "The mutual respect, as well as the genuine fondness between you and the king is obvious."

Honor steps under my arm and straightens on the other side of the obstruction. "That's true. I love my brother. I'm simply confused by him right now."

Lukas ducks under my arm next and offers me a nod of

thanks. "I think the fastest and easiest way to alleviate that confusion is to spend time with him and his mates. You don't understand how he could love a child and an enemy and yet, you don't know either of them the way he does."

She turns back and frowns. "I understand that, and I'll get there. Right now, I'm more interested in learning about my future. I haven't got the energy for much more than that."

Something passes between the two of them and then she shifts her attention to Dune and me. "Tell me more about yourselves, gentlemen. I feel like there's this awkward neon arrow pointing at me flashing, 'Guardian of the Crown', but I don't know who that is or how to get there. If you are on this ride with me, I'd like to know more about you."

Dune jumps at the opportunity to preen. The male has no problem talking about himself. In fact, in every instance, he struggles to *not* talk about himself.

He spends the next five minutes consuming our time and telling us all about his life in the desert and the life he had prior to becoming an Amberloq trainee.

"And you have no idea who your biological mother or father is?" Honor asks, stepping over a fallen log that's gone pithy in the middle.

"Biological? No. That's not how the desert nomad society works. The women run things and until we're old enough to either serve the crown or the tribe, all of them are our mothers. They take positions within the group based on their strengths and passions and everyone contributes to the whole."

"How does that work?" Lukas asks.

"Well... for example, my mothers Havva and Rivka are the best cooks of my tribe, and their contribution is to assure the meals are prepared and our family is fed. My mothers Elia, Rahil, and Yudit are the caregivers. They raise and bathe us and watch over us as we grow."

Honor frowns at a stone wall heavily overgrown with ivy

and leaves. It's an imposing height and seems to run the entire perimeter of the Amberloq compound.

After thinking about it for a moment, she starts pulling at the greenery to clear a path. "And if you weren't an Amberloq warrior, what choices do the men have within your system. What would you have been?"

I grunt. "Don't you dare say you would've been a procreator."

Dune sets down his cooler of food and helps the princess unearth an old, iron gate. "No. All the men lay with the females. There's no designation for that."

"What about love and commitment?" Honor asks. "Does anyone in your tribe opt for a more traditional relationship?"

Dune laughs. "That *is* our tradition. I suppose if they wanted a more urban, modern relationship, they could pair off and move to the city, but why? Our way of living allows everyone to do the things they love and be the person that brings them happiness. Our entire societal structure is based on love and commitment."

"It's funny," Honor says. "I always knew a multiple mating was part of my position, but it seems odd to think about Creed sharing his heart with three people... especially after living in the Human Realm with Calli for what felt like ten years of dating in that society."

Lukas chuckles. "Six months ago, I found the idea of polyamorous marriage very strange. After seeing Hawk come into his own, my mind has broadened. The way the members of the quint interact and support one another is amazing. I gotta say, I see the plus side."

"Sexually, you mean?" Honor says.

He shakes his head. "No. It's like Dune said about his community, with the quint, everyone has different strengths and the contributions strengthen the whole. They've got Hawk's need to plan and control, Calli's sass and charm, Kotah's calming patience, Brant's easygoing humor, and Jaxx's strength in focusing them and keeping them on course. It works for them and they excel because of it."

I grunt pulling the gate free from any strangling vines. Lukas's stance on things surprises me. The man is aggressive and possessive. When we arrived, he was downright hostile about us being part of Honor's life.

Or that's the way I took it while he was discharging his weapon at me.

"Press your palm over the security screen, Princess," Lukas says. "While you were in your room thinking, I had Rhylan reinstate your past security scan at the highest clearance level."

Honor looks truly pleased as she passes her hand over the scanner.

Click. The gate latch releases.

The four of us step inside the barrier of the thick, stone wall and I take in the vast but neglected grounds. Amberloq Hall is a place of historic importance that I've only heard stories of since I was a boy.

Now I have the chance to see it and possibly be part of the revival of it.

"I'm sorry to be the one to say it," Dune says, "but I am underwhelmed. This place is a dump."

Honor sighs. "It is right now, yes, but Calli isn't the only one who can rise from the ashes. We've got to dig in and course-correct what happened all those years ago with my father and my aunt."

"What did happen?" Lukas asks. "You've mentioned a falling out, but you've never said more."

"That's because I'm not sure of all the details and what I do know, I'm not sure you want to hear."

His brow creases. "What does that mean?"

Honor glances at the three of us and seems to decide that it's a conversation we can all be involved in. "You boys served under her, so you are aware my aunt took a stance against bonding with her generals."

I nod. "It wasn't spoken about often, but it was generally known. She had Erickson and accepted no other into her bed or her heart."

Honor nods. "She chose him over her duty to unite the biomes of the quadrant."

Lukas frowns. "And you think that was part of the downfall of the Amberloq?"

"My father always said the generals never felt they were being given equal consideration. The joining, as you saw, is both physical and magical. Our bond will grow and we will become one unit."

"And you think that will upset me?"

"Well, doesn't it?"

He tilts his head from side to side. "I admit, when I first learned of what is expected of you, it took me back. But I'm a progressive thinker and like I said, over the past six months I've watched two very successful polyamorous relationships take hold. I think what the quint has and what your brother has is astounding."

I catch Dune's glare and shake my head.

This is not our place to interject.

"And you're open to something like that?"

He shrugs. "Open, yes, but I think it's too early in the game to start making those kinds of decisions. You're still finding your footing. There's no reason to foist undue pressure on you. Focus on restoring the Amberloq presence in the quadrant and see where we land."

"But you're committed to helping with that?"

"I am."

"We all are, Princess," Dune says, inserting himself. "We will do whatever is asked of us—except cleaning toilets. I hate cleaning toilets. Tundra is up for anything though, aren't you buddy? Toilets and all."

The three of us ignore him and go back to studying our surroundings. With the amount of overgrowth and forest debris, it's hard to imagine this property ever held a place of honor in our quadrant.

"What are we looking at, exactly?" Lukas asks. "Where should we start?"

"The main building is the home and office of the fighting force," Honor says, pointing at the stone, four-story building straight ahead of us. "That building over there is the training pavilion and that structure by the pond is the meditation temple."

"How many warriors used to serve the crown?" Lukas asks.

Honor looks to me to answer. "The largest army recorded was active during the Wars of Power when there were over three hundred warriors. When Laryssa attacked, our numbers were half that."

Lukas grips the strap of his duffle bag and pulls it higher onto his shoulder. "From three hundred to two. I'd say we've got our work cut out for us."

"We?" Dune scowls, his wings ruffling behind him in the breeze. "Being an Amberloq isn't a self-appointed position."

"Dune, mind your words," I say, not liking his tone.

Dune shakes his head and gestures between Lukas and Princess Honor. "You two have something sexual happening, that's obvious, but you are a human who serves another king in another realm. You say you're here to help but you aren't part of our *we*."

He holds his hand out and gestures between himself, Honor, and me. "*We* are the *we*. You have been a useful if not overbearing military consultant up until this point but you're not Amberloq and never will be."

Lukas blinks. "And you are little more than an opportunistic, childish dick, who got here by default."

Dune's wings flare and he launches forward, pumping his wings and catching Lukas around the ribs. They collide with a solid *thunk* and then the two fly backward.

Dune slams him into the trunk of a tree.

And then Lukas blasts him with an explosion of blue magic. Dune is shot backward and topples head over heels through the air toward the pond.

With enough distance between them to get in the middle, Honor and I step in to stop the conflict.

"Don't! Stop this!" Honor raises her hands, standing between them, and glares at first Dune and then Lukas. "We have actual enemies to fight. We don't need to fight amongst ourselves."

"You're right, Princess," Dune says, spitting mad. "Maybe it's time your boyfriend takes his leave so we can focus on Amberloq business."

"Dune, enough," I snap. "You overstep."

Dune scowls at me. "Come on, Tundra. You can't honestly think he belongs here with us?"

Both Honor and Lukas shift their gaze to me. "It is not my place to voice an opinion."

"No, go ahead," Lukas says, stepping back. "Let's hear it. Do you agree with Dune? I don't have feathers so I'm not part of this?"

I frown. "It has nothing to do with feathers."

"But?"

"But the traditions of the Amberloq are something I value. The testings. The qualifiers. The trials. This is the sacred hall for an organization I've dedicated my life to. Even if you excel in military leadership, that isn't transferable. Amberloq Hall is meant for Amberloq warriors and you are not one."

He scrubs a hand over his face, his breathing rough. "So, I'm not Amberloq so I have no business being here, is that it?"

"I didn't say that."

"Oh, I think that's exactly what you're saying." He turns and looks at Honor. "Is that the way you feel?"

Honor swallows, looking torn. "You have been my rock since I woke up. You're an incredible man and a treasured support, but they aren't completely off-base. I wasn't thinking about it like that, but yeah, Amberloq Hall holds certain traditions."

The words strike him as brutally as a physical blow and when he reels, Honor realizes it.

She throws her hands up and steps closer. "They aren't completely right either. You have never overstepped and I think your qualifications absolutely give you the right to—"

He holds his hands up refusing to let her touch him.

His jaw twitches as he grinds his molars together. Stepping back, he lets his duffle slide off his shoulder and hands it to me. "Please return my tools when you're finished with them."

Honor tries again to reach him, but he avoids her touch. "But this was your idea. What about exploring and rebuilding? We can make our own traditions. I don't want to exclude you."

Lukas straightens to his full height and lifts his chin. "This is Amberloq Hall and as you each have pointed out, I'm not Amberloq and never will be. You're not excluding me, I'm removing myself. I leave you three to your destiny. Excuse me."

CHAPTER FIFTEEN

Honor

"What the hell just happened?" I look from Tundra to Dune and back to the iron gate swinging open as Lukas storms off into the trees. How did things go from the four of us bonding to the two of us breaking up in a matter of minutes?

Wait, is that what happened?

Did we break up?

Were we even officially together?

"If I can make a suggestion without overstepping, Princess," Tundra says, quietly beside me. "Go after him. It's obvious he cares deeply for you and was hurt by what was said. In my experience, wounds are best closed quickly before too much blood is lost."

I hate that Lukas is hurt, but what would I say differently? Dune might be tactless, but he has a point. I can't condemn Valorous for disregarding Amberloq traditions for the sake of a lover and then turn around and do the same thing.

I need to respect the viewpoint of my generals.

I need to focus on reviving the home base.

I need to re-establish ourselves as a credible force.

That is my priority.

Not following my heart or putting myself before my duty. That's what Valorous did and we all paid the price.

The Guardian of the Crown serves the people.

Walking over to the gate, I stare into the darkness and then click the gate closed. "I appreciate your counsel, Tundra, but for tonight, we'll focus on rediscovering Amberloq Hall and forming a plan for future efforts."

Tundra nods. "As you wish, Princess."

With that, I get us back on track.

It takes a bit of effort to get across the ground and onto the deep porch that wraps around the stone manse, but once we're there, it's the work of a moment to get inside. I wipe off the security scanner beside the door and it opens without hesitation.

It was thoughtful of Lukas to have my security clearance programmed into the system.

He is an amazing intelligence and security officer.

"He never overstepped," I say, sighing. "Dune, you were wrong about that. Lukas has only ever been supportive and helpful to me and, by extension, to us."

"Yes, Princess. I *am* sorry I've caused you pain. I'm accustomed to people being angry at me, but I never meant to hurt you or make things more difficult for you in this already difficult time."

"I appreciate that, Dune. Thank you." I meet the man's gaze and draw a deep breath. "Enough of personal issues. We came to evaluate our starting point for pulling our lives back together. Let's focus."

"Yes, Princess."

"And please, both of you, call me Honor. However, things play out, we've been paired together going forward. We might as well get used to interacting with one another as friends and colleagues and start building those bonds."

Dune dips his chin, his sandy blond hair falling forward around his rich, brown horns. "Where do we start?"

I scratch my cheek. "This place is a dump—you weren't wrong—but having seen what it was, I know what it can be again. Spread out, pick a room and let's see what we can get done.

The boys set the supplies down in the expansive entranceway and we all wander a bit, assessing where things stand. As a girl growing up in the shadow of the great Valorous, I used to think it was sad that things fell apart the way they did.

As an adult inheriting her legacy, I'm pissed.

She ruined the system that the foundation of our quadrant is built upon and then went off and got herself killed leaving me to clean up her mess?

Talk about arrogant.

Maybe she was a great leader of the Amberloq warriors, but they were supposed to be serving the citizens of Dornte not becoming an elite army separated from the people and their needs.

It was stupid. It was selfish.

And it's not how things are going to go this time.

Lukas

Sticks snap under my boots as I tromp through the forest and return to the castle. I can't decide who I'm angriest at, Dune for being a fucking ass, Tundra for being shortsighted, Honor for agreeing with them, me for falling for the sweet and sappy shit, or Shadow for jinxing me with that bullshit about not getting involved because we'd slip into an unhealthy protector dependency.

Shadow. This is definitely Shadow's fault.

I realize he's the least at fault of all of us, but it makes me feel better to point my finger gun at someone.

I'm halfway back to the castle when my wrist communicator goes off. I tilt the face of my watch so I can read the lit-up text.

"Fucking A."

Pulling the datapad from the thigh pocket of my fatigues, I call up Hawk in a video chat and wait for him to come online.

"This better be good," he says, tilting the screen and shifting so his back is toward a wall. It cuts off the room so I can't see anything except his tattooed chest glistening with sweat.

Fuck. Do they ever stop?

"Rhylan has a hit on Hunter's location. Your little brother is ten minutes away at a restaurant in the corridor. I'm meeting the dragon at the pickup loop now."

"I'm coming. Give me two."

I hang up and weave my way out of the forest and around the side of the stone castle. Should I contact Honor and let her know that we're moving on Hunter?

Part of me thinks she should know.

Another part of me feels like being a petty dick and cutting her out of the action.

After all, I'm a human serving another king from another realm. I'm not one of them. I'm not even welcome in their little clubhouse.

When I arrive at the pickup loop at the side of the castle, a concierge pulls up with one of Hawk's surviving SUVs. Good thing he imported six. Two got killed and one severely maimed in their maiden voyage.

"I'll take the keys," I say, jogging to intercept the driver before he heads back into his little hut.

The guy stalls out and clenches his fist around the fob. "Prince Rhylan ordered the vehicle."

"I know, buddy. It's fine. He called me, too. We're going out together. He'll be out in a second and I'll be driving. You're good."

And yet still, he doesn't hand the keys over.

"For fuck's sake," I snap. "Give me the goddamn keys or I'll rip your fingers the fuck off."

I'm not sure what he sees in my expression, but he now looks like he might piss himself. I swipe the keys out of his hand, stomp over to the truck.

The door slams and then I jam the key into the ignition and crank. The engine does its thing and I hit the gas and let the rumble of the motor roar.

"Are we entering a drag race?" Hawk asks, jumping into the back. "I can get Calli to come out and drop a scarf to send us off?"

I don't answer. I glare at him in the rearview as Jaxx climbs in the back next to him and Rhylan slides into the shotgun seat.

I pop the gearshift and pull away, squelching the tires and burning rubber as I go.

"All right," Hawk says. "What happened?"

"Nothing."

"Uh-huh. If you say so."

"I do."

Thankfully, Rhylan is more interested in catching Hunter than my almost love life crashing and burning on the tarmac before even getting lift-off.

The dragon punches the details into the navigation system and the street map pops up with a little red dot indicating our destination. "It works. Excellent."

"I told you it would," Hawk says. "The integration between StoneHaven tech and ours isn't that difficult. You guys, after all, monitored and copied most innovations from our realm."

Rhylan chuckles. "I don't know if I'd go that far. Music, swearing, and stretch pants on women are the biggest innovations we borrowed but that's not what our realm runs on."

Jaxx chuckles. "Although, music, swearin', and stretch pants are some of our best events."

Hawk grins. "That's true. I think women in stretch pants should be what all realms run on."

I fight the roll of my eyes and focus on the road ahead. No sense looking in the rearview. It's the next battle on the horizon that matters.

Yeah, I may have taken a bit of a detour there for a second but that's on me.

From now on, I stay in my lane.

~

Dune

Something tells me I screwed up bigger than usual. As much as I think I was right in what I said to Lukas, now Honor is sad—like really sad. I don't know why that bothers me so much. Everything I said was true.

Lucas isn't one of us.

He doesn't need to be here acting like he is while we figure out how to revive the Amberloq.

When he stormed off, I thought that was a good thing and we'd get things on track—just the three of us. Unfortunately, this was his idea and without him, we're not really sure where to start.

The three of us wander the maze of rooms from floor to floor taking in what was once an amazing home base for an incredible organization.

I'm not sure how it will be that again. There are only three of us and this is a lot of house for three people.

"Honor," Tundra says, exiting a room, which by the rows and rows of empty shelves, I'm guessing was once the library. "I've found something I'd like you to see."

Even though I wasn't involved in the invitation I step out of the small storage room I'm looking at and head back to the library where my white feathered friend is grinning like an idiot.

"What's with the face, Iceman? You look stupid by the way. I don't think smiling is a good look for you."

Tundra scowls. "Try to be nice. We're working on something important here and that means you can't be inciting dissension at every turn."

I know he's right but picking at people and pushing buttons is kind of my thing.

"What have you found?" Honor asks sweeping into the room, her silver braid swinging behind her ass.

Tundra points at a wall cabinet where he unearthed a small security screen. "I found it odd that with all the empty shelves, these books remained. Then I found the scanner and it made more sense."

"How so?"

"An ancient elder in my clan once told me about the Chronicles of the Amberloq and how the stories of our past were stored within a private chamber in the guardian's library. I was searching for a way to access the chamber, and I came up with this. I think it's a DNA scanner and you will be the one able to unlock it."

Honor gives him a warm smile. "Amazing work, Tundra. This is excellent."

I curse myself for a missed opportunity.

How that white-feathered, stick up his ass warrior is making personal inroads with our queen while I'm the source of her sorrow is beyond me.

I'm the good-time guy. I am the one who puts the smiles on the ladies' faces.

True I've never interacted with someone on the level of Princess Honor, but women are all the same, aren't they? I shake myself inwardly and wonder what's going on? In what world does Tundra make headway with a woman while I'm second-guessing myself?

It has been a weird day.

I go over and stand with the two of them, watching as Honor takes a closer look at the scanner. "How do you look at that and come up with DNA scanner? It looks like a small black mirror attached to the wall."

"No, it looks exactly like the DNA scanners we read about in the Science of StoneHaven during our training."

I frown at the black mirror. "I don't see it."

"Did you read the assigned texts?"

"That's beside the point."

Tundra looks at Honor then me. "No. It's exactly the point. You're arguing that it doesn't look like the scanner in the required reading, and you didn't read the text."

I hold up a finger. "I concede, I could have paid more attention during our training, but nobody read all those boring texts assigned to us."

"I did. And yes, everyone else I knew did."

I shrug. "Yeah, well, I worked on other aspects of my training."

"Like using your position to bed women?"

I frown and tilt my head toward Honor. "Now who's not being nice. That was uncalled for."

Honor rolls her eyes and flicks her hand to shoo us back. "Bicker later. Right now, I want to see if Tundra is right and this unlocks something."

Honor reaches to the back of the shelf and presses her hand against the shiny black surface.

The three of us wait, glancing around for a moment, and then a soft *click* sounds somewhere close by.

"What was that?" Honor asks, casting a curious glance around the space. "Where did it come from?"

Tundra steps to the edge of the bookshelf and is leaning to see behind it. With his fingers tracing the seam between the wood and the wall, he frowns. "I'm not sure. It sounded like something unlocking but what and where?"

"Search the room and maybe we'll find out."

Finding the source of the soft click now becomes my goal. I can show Honor I'm an asset to the team.

I have skills.

I focus on finding a hidden passage or maybe the bookshelf swings away or under the floor there might be a loose board where I'll find the hatch to open a cubbyhole…

After ten minutes of searching, I find nothing.

We find nothing.

And then, while we're still looking, the soft *click* sounds again.

Honor looks around and frowns. "What was that?"

"If I were to guess," Tundra says, "I'd say that was the sound of whatever you unlocked relocking because we didn't find it and open it in time. The DNA scanner is likely attached to a timer which resets."

"All right, then I'll activate it again. You boys spread out and see if you can pinpoint where the sound is coming from this time." Honor steps back to the bookshelf and places her hand on the black mirror once again.

Nothing happens.

Her head cranks around as she looks to Tundra for answers. "Why didn't it work?"

The big guy leans in close and looks at the mirror as if that will tell him something. "It's probably part of the timer security.

Since we didn't get it open in time, it probably times out and will reset."

"Reset when?"

He lifts a mighty shoulder and frowns. "I'm sorry, I don't know. It could be an hour it could be a day."

Honor nods, looking disappointed. "Fine, then we'll keep exploring and making a plan about how to revive this place, and try the scanner again before we leave."

Tundra nods. "A fine plan."

"*Kiss ass*," I cough into my hand.

"What was that?" he asks me.

"Oh, nothing. As you were."

He arches an ebony brow and focuses on Honor. "In truth, there is no rush. Whatever secrets hidden in this library have waited for you for twenty years. Whether we find them in an hour or a day or a week they are meant for you. I feel it."

Honor reaches around the warrior and presses her cheek to his as she hugs him. "Thank you, Tundra. I needed to hear that."

CHAPTER SIXTEEN

Lukas

$\mathcal{I}$ pull the truck along the side of the building we believe Hunter entered less than an hour ago. Our spot is close to the exit and I point the tires straight toward the road should we need to make chase or get away, depending on how the evening goes.

"Everyone ready for this?" I ask.

"More than ready," Hawk says. "I've been looking forward to this for months."

The four of us drop out of the truck and take a look at where we are. The place is posh and the line to get in is long, extending down the street and snaking around the corner. Soulful music, elven ballad if I had to make a guess, drifts through blackout windows as well-dressed customers exit with big smiles.

Rhylan slows our stride as we approach the velvet rope and that's likely a good idea. The dragon has a strong, Nordic god kind of frame and when he's barreling at you, even if you know the guy, it's intimidating.

He stops in front of the two professional wrestlers in tuxes and flashes them a heavy gold key. It's not a truck key or anything you'd have hanging on your key ring, but one of those heavy mottled iron keys that could lock the creepy attic of a haunted mansion.

The burly bouncers catch sight of the ancient brass hardware and unhook the barrier. Whatever that key represents, it seems to hold the magic to open our way and grant us immediate entrance.

As curious as I am about that, there's no time to ask him before a hostess in a slinky slip dress meets us at the door. She's a petite thing with jet black hair and pale purple skin. "Do you gentlemen have a booking?"

"No," Rhylan says, waving that key in front of himself. "We're meeting a friend."

The woman lifts her gaze from the electronic blueprint of the place and offers us a patient smile. "I haven't been informed anyone is expecting to be joined by an outside party. I'm sorry, but we respect our clients' privacy. You'll have to contact them and have them come out to claim you."

I grunt and am about to say something when Hawk shakes his head. "Exactly the right answer, Taznia," he says reading the name on the gold and black choker around her throat. "I expect privacy myself. In fact, I had my man pose the question specifically to see how you would respond. Well done."

Hawk pulls out his billfold and takes over the conversation. "You see, I'm new to the quadrant and asked the dragon to take me somewhere I could enjoy some particular comforts."

He peels off a blue note and rolls it into a tube before tucking it into the front of her bra. He lets his hand linger over her cleavage for a moment longer than necessary, but the flirtation is well received.

"I am incredibly interested in having a private tour if you could fit me in."

She seems flustered and checks her watch. "We don't do tours after eight and certainly not group tours."

"Why is that?" he asks.

"Well, for one, we're busy and many of the dining rooms are occupied and won't be available to tour, and also, we don't want to disturb the other patrons."

Hawk smiles, unbuttoning the top two buttons of his fancy dress shirt. The girl gets an eyeful of his tats and nearly orgasms on the spot. "How about this. I'll only take one of my security team with me and ask the other two to wait outside. Then, you can show me around behind the curtain and I promise not to disturb anyone. My life is all about discretion."

She bites her bottom lip practically overdosing on pheromones. "I don't know."

Hawk pulls that billfold out again and peels off the next blue bill. "I would be very grateful, Taznia. So. Very. Grateful."

She swallows and licks her full, pink lips. "All right. If two of you agree to wait outside, I'll get someone to cover the door, and then I'll take you through."

"Perfection," Hawk says.

The moment Taznia ducks through the curtain, Jaxx turns toward us, his eyes wide. "What kind of restaurant is this?"

"The kind that feeds *all* manner of hunger," Hawk says, waggling his brow.

"You picked up on that quickly," Rhylan says.

"Expensive atmosphere, blackout windows, a line around the block of people panty-damp and aching to get inside. As Jaxx would say, this ain't my first rodeo."

"His either, it seems," I add, pointing at Rhy.

"Sorry, you read me wrong. This is not my scene."

Jaxx chuckles. "Says the male with the VIP passkey in his pocket. I didn't peg you for the lifestyle dragon."

Rhylan's frown grows more severe. "Is this going to become a thing and bite me in the ass?"

Hawk shakes his head. "Not if you don't do anything outside of your marital bonds, no."

The dragon shakes his head. "This place is solidly in my past. Vik liked to come here and I liked to forget how slecked up my life was. That was then. I know what I've got going on."

"How is that twin of yours?" Jaxx says. "Have you made any inroads with him and your clan now that your mama runs the show?"

"Not a one. Now, who's going in and who's waiting at the truck?"

Hawk takes the hint and accepts the change of subject. "Jaxx and Rhylan cover the exit. Lukas and I will search in here."

I toss Rhylan the keys as Jaxx sticks his bottom lip out. "Aw... I was lookin' forward to seein' you in your element, hotness. How did I not make the shortlist? I give you sexual favors."

Hawk flashes him a gaze filled with all kinds of heated promises. "We'll borrow Rhy's VIP key one night and pop back for a night on the town. Promise."

A deep-throated purr hits the air and Jaxx smiles. "Done deal."

The two of them share a look and it's obvious they're talking cranium-to-cranium.

Seriously. Do they ever stop? People in love suck.

Jaxx ends the private convo by gripping both of Hawk's shoulders and bracing himself in front of his mate. "Resist temptation, hotness. You can get through this unscathed. Just remember, your mates are your outlet now."

Hawk chuckles. "Fuck off and go. If you're lucky I'll scare the little chicken out of the hen house and your jaguar can snap him up in his sharp teeth."

Jaxx snaps his teeth. "You say the nicest things."

I roll my eyes as Jaxx and Rhy turn to step outside... "Come, Dragon. Looks like we get to enjoy the summer night."

Honor

Dune, Tundra, and I do what we can to clean up Amberloq Hall and I'm daunted by what a big job this will be. Exhausted and deflated, the three of us close things up and head back to the castle proper.

"How long do you think it will take us before we're able to move in?" Dune asks.

I shrug. "I don't know. I suppose if we focus on cleaning up a few of the bedrooms and a bathroom, we could be settled in a couple of days."

"Bedrooms… plural? Sooner if we shared, yeah?"

I meet the teasing gaze of my desert warrior. Between his sculpted features and the warm tone of his skin, it's easy to imagine him in some erotic fantasy.

My mind fae energy kicks in and I picture him racing into my oasis camp naked on horseback. Clad only in scant leather armor. He kicks his leg over the beast and dismounts before his horse even stops kicking up sand.

He's so eager to ravish me.

I swallow, pushing down the deep need aching inside me. The magic of the joining is taking hold but then I think about Lukas and all the days and nights he eased me as my sexy shadow.

And then this afternoon in our brick hiding spot.

My need kicks in and my heart aches.

"Yes, plural. Either that or we can stay in my suite, and you can couch surf. Or, if not, I can get you into one of the guest suites."

Tundra dips his chin. "We are happy to remain in the suite with you for however long it takes. And separate rooms are fine. We have a lifetime to find our rhythm. There's no need to rush."

A fleeting thought points out that after our heated parting, we might get back to the suite to find that Creed's room is cleared out and vacant.

My lungs are lead, the weight on my chest crushing.

Why does it feel like if I don't make things right with Lukas ASAP, I'll regret it for the rest of my life?

"It'll work out, Princess. You'll see." Tundra's voice is deep and gentle. He catches my wrist and pulls me to a stop on the overgrown path. "Lukas is both intelligent and strategic. He knows what a treasure you are. He also knows you haven't found your footing yet. He'll forgive the damage to his heart."

I swipe at the tears warming my cheeks and sigh. "He shouldn't have suffered damage to his heart. He's done nothing but be one-hundred percent amazing and supportive. I don't care that he's not Amberloq. Maybe our way forward is to build a broader foundation."

"Perhaps it is. Propose that to him. I bet he's just as forlorn and out of sorts as you are."

I let Tundra pull me against his chest and wrap my arms around his hips. He smells of crisp mountain air and I breathe him into the depth of my lungs.

Soft-spoken and sharp-witted, my general from the frozen planes flirts in a subtle, subdued way that Dune could never manage. My iceman, as Dune calls him, has a sadness in his eyes that suggests he understands being hurt too well.

I squeeze him tighter. "Thank you, Tundra."

Easing back, he winks. "If it means anything to you, I think you are amazing and will rise to be twice the Amberloq leader your aunt was."

I draw a steadying breath and wipe away the last of my tears. "From your lips to the gods' ears."

The three of us walk together until we exit the forested area at the back of the castle, and I pause. "I'm going to visit my brother and check on Shadow in the King's Tower. You two take Lukas's tools back to his room and have the first showers. I'll get cleaned up once I get back."

"Do you want us to come with you?" Dune asks.

"No. It'll be good for me to spend some time with Creed and his mates alone."

Lukas wanted me to do that from the start, but I wasn't ready.

Or at least I *said* I wasn't ready.

In truth, I was hurt and angry.

As Dune and Tundra make their way to the back entrance of the castle, I walk around toward the north tower to where the royal residence is located.

With each step I take toward my childhood home, I feel wearier and wearier.

It really is over.

My family. My parents. My life as it used to be.

I've known that logically for years but the little girl that used to run these halls like a wild child and dream of becoming a great warrior hadn't accepted it.

As I trudge up the landscaped lawn, I nod to the guard at the entrance and stall out. Maybe I should come back tomorrow when everyone is rested. Maybe arriving unannounced is rude. They are, after all, newlyweds.

Yeah... I should come back.

I turn to leave and am struck hard from behind.

The crack to my head and left shoulder knocks me to the ground.

"End this," someone says above me. "Take her out."

The phrase strikes a chord, and it dawns on me that the attackers in the cobbled courtyard said the same thing. I thought Keyla was the target.

Was it me all along?

My vision is still black and spotty when they close in. Pushing off the manicured grass, I scramble to get to my feet at the same time three goblins come at me.

One grabs each of my arms and the third comes at me with a syringe injector.

Fuck that.

Using the ones securing me by the arms as an anchor, I mule kick my legs, flicking them high and hard into the air. I catch Dr. Doom in the chest and knock him flying backward. "Guards! Help!"

The grip on my arms is bruisingly tight and I'm no closer to escaping the hold by the time the male with the syringe composes himself and comes at me again.

Where the hell is the palace guard?

As I flip and twist, I look over my shoulder and curse at the man heaped at the castle entrance.

"Guards!"

Reaching out with my gift, I try to connect with their mental pathways and shut them down. Nothing happens. Dammit.

Creed has always been better at mental offense than me. I try again and a shooting pain pierces my skull.

I double forward, blood dripping down my lip.

The man in front of me with the auto-injector chuckles. "Your mind tricks won't work on us, Princess. We can block your assault."

Well, shit.

Maybe if I were at my peak and rested, I could defend myself against these three but this is not the time. After the coma and the explosion... the most I can hope for is making it difficult for them and hope someone comes to my aid.

My muscles burn with fatigue and my kicks are growing increasingly sloppy. When Dr. Doom comes at me this time, I don't have the strength to fight him off.

"Hold her."

The feral growl of wild animals comes a moment before two

massive wolves come flying out of the forest and launch into the air.

On a full run with teeth bared, Keyla's stunning white wolf and a beautiful chocolate brown and silver wolf charge my attackers. Without hesitation, the two of them tear into the goblins.

Knocked to the ground, I take a much-needed breath and search the area to call for help.

No need.

The door to the royal tower bursts open and Dillan and Brant come racing out. They start my way on two feet and then launch forward shifting into their animal forms on the fly.

I sag to the grass, the battle all but over.

CHAPTER SEVENTEEN

Dune

It takes a bit to get the stench of burning oil out of my feathers but after I finish in the washroom and towel dry, I head out to the living room with a towel wrapped around my hips.

Tundra is sitting on the couch, freshly washed, with his wings extended along the back cushions to dry his feathers. With no shirt on and those white wings of his spread wide, he's looking good.

I might go out of my way to antagonize the guy, but I'll never complain about the view. He's got the whole sexy as sin thing going on.

"Don't look at me like that."

I chuckle and lift my palms. "As of a few weeks ago, this is once again a free realm. You might outrank me in all things duty-bound, but I don't think you have the power to control who I look at or how. Besides, if you don't want me to look, why pose?"

Tundra rolls his eyes and rises from the couch. "I wasn't posing. I was air-drying my wings."

"Uh-huh, if you say so. Both of us know the truth."

Tundra throws his leather vest over his head and twists to secure the side straps. "And what truth is that?"

I frown at him. "Don't bother standing there pretending there's nothing between us except a shared position as one of the generals."

"There's not."

"What about what went down on the mountain?"

He frowns. "Nothing went down on the mountain."

I bark a laugh. "There's no way you can say that to me with a straight face."

"The retreat is a place for reflection and introspection. It is a safe place for self-discovery and expanding boundaries."

"Well, your self-discovery included wrapping your lips around my cock and both of us getting dark and dirty with each other in every boundary expanding way."

He turns and glares at me. "We were left on that mountain with no idea the world had changed. After the first year, I would've fucked a watermelon if it smiled at me. Desperation breeds poor judgment. I refuse to be judged on that."

"It's you who's judging." I chuckle, tugging the tail of my towel free from its tuck. "You're telling me that months of us screwing around meant nothing beyond scratching an itch and that I don't even rank higher than garden produce."

He sighs, turning to stare at me. "That's what I'm saying. I apologize if it came out like a judgment. That's not what I meant. I simply want to be clear with you."

Gripping both ends of the towel, I open the flaps of fabric and take a step closer. "So, to be clear... you're saying there was nothing beyond the mechanics involved and I don't affect you at all."

"That's what I'm saying," he says, grabbing the pillow I used last night off the floor and setting it on the back of the couch.

I toss my towel onto the pile and stroke a hand under my cock. "So, it does nothing for you to know my balls are tingling just thinking about how we spent time on that mountain."

"No, it doesn't."

"So, when you stroke yourself at night you don't think about my hot mouth sucking you off and swallowing your cum as you lose your mind?"

"You need to stop."

I stroke my length from base to tip and back again, sweeping my free hand across my abs and up to my pec. "I think you need to let off some steam, T. You gotta release some of that pressure you put on yourself or you're gonna self-destruct."

He swallows and strides off, his feathers ruffling as he grabs the cooler bag with the packed snacks and retreats down the hall to the kitchen.

I follow, stalking him, priming my erection as I pad along behind him naked. "I'm serious. You're wound up and need to let off some steam."

"No. What happened on that mountain stayed on that mountain. It's humiliating enough to know we missed the end of the world because we were being punished like children. It's worse to know we spent all that time up there when we were needed here."

"We're here now."

He shoves the bag onto the counter and turns on me. "Doesn't it bother you that we could've been the two that made the difference? Maybe we could've freed Valorous from her imprisonment before she was murdered. How many months did she sit in captivity expecting us to save her?"

"That is *not* on us. The last thing she said to us was, 'Go to the mountain and stay there until I send for you.' Well, she never sent for us, and so we stayed up there."

"Put some clothes on."

I step back from the counter so my full-frontal is visible to him. Grinning, I point to the front of his pants and smile at the bulge pressing on the fabric. "Deny it all you want. Part of you loved what we got up to on that mountain."

"I hate you."

My cock kicks against my palm. "Yeah, you do. Come show me how much."

"No. Not here. This is our lady's home."

I reach into the cupboard and pull out the vegetable oil. Opening the lid, I pour a pool in the palm of my hand and then rub my hands together. One hand slicks the front and the other takes care of the back.

"She's visiting with her brother and Shadow. Lukas won't be back any time soon. We have time."

"No." He moves to step toward the doorway, and I block his retreat. "We've danced this dance enough times to know where we'll end up. You've got serious tension to let off and we both know how to best get you leveled out."

"Get out of my way, Dune."

"Make me."

He moves to push past, and I press my oily hands against his chest. Gripping the leather of his vest, I swing him around and slam his back against the wall. Pushing forward, I claim his mouth. Pressed full-bodied against him, I am achingly aware of every hot, hard, chiseled inch of him.

I distantly register him protesting my advance before his resistance breaks and he's kissing me back like he wants to eat me alive.

This is the side of Tundra others don't get to see.

Beneath the soft-spoken calm and control, he's aggressive and wild.

With a hiss and a curse, he grips my hips and stares at me, his gaze searingly intense. "You are such a pain in my ass."

"Why don't you repay me and even the score."

There's a moment of hesitation when I wonder if he'll walk away from this but then he grips my throat and kisses me back. Tundra's kiss is neither calm nor controlled. It is a full-on, tongue invasion with that big body of his pressing an erection the size of a nightstick against my navel.

For once... I'm not complaining.

When he spins me and shoves me up against the marble countertop of the island, I spread my wings and my legs, bracing for what's coming.

This is what Tundra is best at.

A zipper undoes behind me and then his pants pool to the floor with a soft thud.

I secure a white-knuckled grip on the countertop and hold on for dear life.

The level of power and hunger Tundra can draw on when he's wound up like this is hard to imagine... unless you've been on the receiving end before.

A rough hand between my shoulder blade pins me face down on the counter and then the crown of his cock pushes and probes my ass.

My breathing quickens to a pant as my oiled-up chest squeaks on the marble surface.

"Do you have any idea how much you piss me off?"

The husky growl in his voice zings hot straight to my sac. "Show me."

The penetration is fast and very deep. Tundra is big and I pushed him far enough that he doesn't care to be gentle. The burn is intense, and the pounding will be just as violent.

I love it.

He's been edgy with me since the magic of our general's call first ignited and we were drawn here.

That's a lot of pent-up frustration.

That's a lot of really good fucking.

He shifts his hands to my hips and the ride and glide rachets up and goes off the rails. I turn my face to the side, grunting and gripping the counter with every thrust.

Movement catches my attention and I find our reflection in the high-gloss polish of the fridge. With his wings outstretched and a look of possessed passion on his face, Tundra is breathtaking.

I bite back the orgasm tingling in my balls.

Closing my eyes, I focus on not ejaculating down the dark-stained cabinets. When you're having the sex of your life, you do your best to never let it end.

Tundra

Down the rabbit hole we go. Again. Dammit, how did I let him get so deep under my skin? Sure, seeing him naked got me aroused—very aroused, but driving him hard out in the open like this? In the kitchen of Honor's apartment? Where anyone can walk in on us?

I am seriously out of my mind.

But having him taunt me, looking at me like he does... my body responded unbidden. And then, with the annoyance, and frustration, and exhaustion of a long, hard day, suddenly there was nothing I wanted more than the mind-numbing pleasure of burying my cock inside him and punishing him for it all.

The thick muscle of my legs is burning but that doesn't slow me down. I piston our lower bodies together, lost in the decadence of familiarity.

Which I hate as much as I love.

Almost.

I spoke the truth. I regret that the two of us spent so many months bickering and having hate sex while our world burned down and we didn't know it.

But I loved it too.

I'd never admit it to him, but he is everything I wish I could be—easygoing, carefree, at peace with who he is.

And who he is—the Dune I know—is much more than the brash and sassy warrior with an over-inflated opinion of himself. He's more than that... he just doesn't want people to realize it.

I realize it.

I see him.

Brushing a hand down the line of his spine, I trace the flex and release of his back muscles and exhale. He's a beautifully made warrior. From the chiseled cut of his jaw to the sculpted muscles of his physique, to the dimpled rounds of his ass.

And when his wings are spread for me as they are, it's the most erotic thing I've ever—

The orgasm that pours out of me is soul-shattering. I arch my back, my breath escaping in heavy bursts. This is the agony and ecstasy of life with Dune. And as much as I protest, there's no question in my mind we'll end up here again.

As I retract from him, cold air chills my heated cock and I shiver. Lowering myself to take a knee, I squeeze his hips and urge him to turn for me.

"I was rough. Let me make it up to you."

He grips my horns with gentle hands and aligns his body up to my mouth. "If you insist."

The teasing triumph in his tone is both annoying and endearing. He knew we'd end up here.

We always do.

Lukas

Taznia takes Hawk and me on a guided tour through the public areas of an adult lifestyle restaurant and club. Dinner and a show, one might say.

And it is quite a show.

Having been Hawk's right hand for over a decade, I've seen a lot of kinky shit. I've been to a lot of private places. And I've never really seen the appeal.

Sure there's the titillation of watching pretty people doing naughty things to one another, but I'm not one for the crowd.

To each their own.

"And this is our VIP lounge," Taznia says, pointing to a closed, red curtain. "It's theme is set up based on the booking of the night. It can be more of a Greco-Roman lounge with a feeding table in the middle and platform benches all around, or a play dungeon, or any number of other themes depending on the number of people and the interest of the party."

Hawk nods. "So, this is the room where someone of my endless means might bring political allies or guests to the realm once things get finalized with the portal gate to the Human Realm."

Taznia's face lights up. "That's why you look so familiar. You're part of the Phoenix Quint. I've seen you on data streams. You're establishing the travel between realms."

He nods. "Exactly, so you understand why I might need a place for selective tastes where I can be assured my privacy and anonymity will be respected."

She nods. "Absolutely. Come, I'll show you the showers and hot jet pool."

"That would be perfect."

As Taznia steps off to continue the tour, Hawk signals me to fall back and start a private search. And yeah, I agree with him, this VIP lounge sounds like it's exactly the place we'll find Hunter and his supporters.

The sound of male laughter approaching the curtain has me

stepping back and turning the corner to avoid being seen. The man who exits is obviously a goblin.

Even wearing a gray cloak with the hood up, there's no disguising the guy's long nose and the ears coming six inches off the side of his head.

The man flags down an employee working the hall and "We're ready for the entertainment to arrive."

"Right away, sir. I'll let them know."

As the woman rushes off to get the party started inside, the goblin returns to the VIP room, and I catch the edge of the curtain as it falls back into place.

A quick peek inside tells me several things.

The room is set up like a gothic castle with an altar table and six men in gray cloaks standing around drinking out of gemmed goblets. It's very World of Warcraft, so I can only imagine what the entertainment will be.

Half naked warrior women in breastplates?

Unfortunately, the cloaks make it nearly impossible to see who's who. I listen to the voices and yeah, I recognize Hunter's haughty laugh.

A soft shuffle behind me has me ducking back down the side hall again as the entertainment arrives.

Yep. Half-naked women in breastplates. Nailed it.

Once they pass, I am ready to go find Hawk.

The tackle comes hard and fast from behind. I hit the tile floor hard but get my hands under me so I don't crack my face. Even as I'm absorbing the fall, I'm rolling to the side to keep from getting pinned.

Fuck this guy's strong.

Fighting my way free from the grapple, I throw my elbow back and curse as the strike hits solid muscle.

Who the hell is this guy?

I'm flipped on my ass and the muzzle of a SIG sauer comes up and starts firing. I curse, gripping the gun with both hands and fighting to keep it from pointing at me.

We wrestle, scrambling and struggling to gain control of the gun. I plant the soles of my boots and buck my hips, launching my robed attacker over my head.

Neither of us lets go of the gun, so I'm dragged along in his wake.

Our fight takes us crashing through the velvet curtain into the VIP room and that's when the world goes to shit.

The women who just arrived start screaming and running in every direction, followed by the men in cloaks scattering like rats abandoning a sinking ship.

"Hunter's on the way out, boys. Don't lose him. I'm blown."

The gun goes off again and I curse. The muzzle was right beside my ear and now my world is ringing like a motherfucker.

Bringing my knee up, I sac the guy hard and he flips back to cup his nuts.

The hood slides off his face and I curse. "You piece of shit. You're still on the wrong side."

"Says you, asshole."

It's jarring to see Rhylan's face on the man trying to kill me. "Your twin is ten times the male you are."

Rolling to the side, I grab one of those massive goblets and crack Vik in the head with the base. He tips to the side and I'm out from under him.

I grab his gun, kick him back to the ground as he tries to push up on his knees, and rush out of the room.

Hawk runs crashing into me and then the two of us are joining the chaotic exodus. "Where'd Hunter go?"

"No idea. I got jumped by Vikarus and the room scattered."

We join the adrenaline-fueled craze and end up in the parking lot looking at an empty parking spot.

"I take it they went after him," I say, my breath heaving in and out.

"Let's hope they catch him."

I lean on the wall, my muscles shaking from one hell of a wrestling match. "Fuck me, fighting a dragon isn't fun."

Hawk is staring at me funny and frowns. "No. I don't suppose it would be."

My legs give way and I'm disoriented enough to look around, wondering what happened.

"Fuck." Hawk takes a knee beside me and lays me flat on the sidewalk. "You're hit, my friend. Lay still. Let me get pressure on this."

He rips the shirt off his back and presses the wad of fabric against the hole in my chest. My head lolls to the side and I watch buttons bounce on the asphalt and across the parking lot.

And then I black the fuck out.

CHAPTER EIGHTEEN

Tundra

$\mathcal{A}$fter an excruciating morning workout with Brant, Doc, and Jaxx the three of them head back to the suites, and Dune and I stay to run a few more miles on the treadmill. Honor attacked. Lukas shot. Convoy blown to bits. We are scrambling to react to the assaults against us but that needs to change.

Dune and I finally agree on something.

Someone standing against Creed's rule targeted Honor. They want to 'take her out.' That isn't going to happen. We need to be better prepared before the next attack. We need to work together and strengthen our team.

Sadly, it isn't a question of *if* there will be another attack, it's only about preparing for when it happens.

I'm still thinking about how close we got to losing Honor last night when Rhylan passes the open door and continues walking down the corridor toward the Dornte security office in the lower level of the castle.

"Rhylan, have you got a minute?" I turn off the machine, hop down, and grab a workout towel to dry off my face and arms.

The dragon hears me call his name and stops, backpedaling toward the gym. "Yeah, I've got a few while I wait for Lukas and Hawk to get down here for an interrogation. Why?"

I catch up with him and gesture for him to continue with his original course. "Several reasons. First off, I want to follow up on the attack on Honor and find out what you've learned from the goblins captured."

"Not much. The facial recognition programs are still running, but they certainly aren't cooperating. Whoever is pulling their strings either has their loyalty or is more dangerous and intimidating than us."

After seeing the dragon in action, it's hard to imagine anyone more intimidating. Loyalty is likely the cause for the interrogation standoff.

"Dune has training in interrogation, would it be all right if we speak to them then?"

"You're a General of the Crown. That is your right."

"Thank you. In that same vein, we'd like to understand more about the technology in the security office and become proficient in running the war table."

"There will be formalities to address to gain you access, but we can work toward that."

"Also, I've been talking with Dune, and we want to find other Amberloq warriors who might be alive or who have come of age in the past two years. Having a military force of two isn't much of a force and now that we're working on restoring Amberloq Hall, we'd like to fill the rooms once the place is functional."

He tilts his head toward the end of the hall and resumes walking. "Come inside, we'll see what we can find out."

After he unlocks the security protocols, he leads the way in. I follow, eyeing up the scanner and keypad as I pass through the door. "Dune and I should be scanned in for access to this room. We are, after all, crown security."

Rhylan strides over to the war table and starts things up. "I agree, but as I mentioned, there are protocols and a series of background questions and assessment forms for you both to fill out before you're given the keycodes and access. It's standard stuff, but important. Once those are in and I verify everything, I'll raise your clearance and grant you access."

The warrior in me balks at needing to prove myself for a position of destiny. It's a slap to my honor. The officer in me understands the precaution.

The dragon is not only a head of castle security, he's also mated to the royal couple.

It makes perfect sense that he wants to know who will be involved in assuring their safety in the future.

Dune steps through the door behind us and glances around the room. "We should have access and be part of this process going forward."

I smile. "We were discussing that prior to your arrival. Once we tell Rhylan a bit more about ourselves and he has a chance to verify our credentials, we'll be one step closer to re-establishing the presence of the Amberloq at the castle."

Dune nods. "Good. Until that happens, maybe you can ensure we're kept in the communication channels. If there are people actively trying to destabilize Dornte's ruling order who are brazen enough to attack Honor on the grounds of Thornebane Castle, we need to be aware of what's going on."

"I have no objection to that. The more the merrier."

Except Dune doesn't look merry. "Jaxx mentioned the two of you went out with Lukas and Hawk last night to apprehend the man suspected of supplying the rebel plot with weapons. Considering the missiles that nearly killed us yesterday, and the bullets we were dodging, we should've been included in that before your in-laws from the other realm."

Rhylan stills and focuses his gaze on Dune. "The man in question is Hawk's half-brother. He and Lukas know him best. It was logical for me to include them in the raid. They also know more about the weaponry that has been smuggled into the quadrant and how to respond to it to keep from getting killed."

"We heard Lukas was shot during the takedown."

Rhylan nods. "Thankfully, he'll make a complete recovery. How's Honor this morning?"

"She was sleeping when we left. There are extra guards on the suite corridor and Calli is watching over her while we're out."

"Good. I'll update Creed. I know he's worried."

Understandably so.

"Is it true that it was your twin who shot him?" Dune asks, catching us both off guard.

The dragon's posture stiffens. "Seems so."

Dune has the good sense to drop that line of questioning.

"Where is Lukas now?" I ask, giving them both an opportunity to change the subject.

"I took him back to the King's Tower after he was cleared by the med-techs. Added him to Doc's patient list so we could keep an eye on him."

That's good.

Had Lukas been killed after their falling out, Honor would've suffered a great deal of guilt and pain. "Going forward, we would like to be included in all quadrant security matters. Princess Honor will assume her position over the next days and weeks and we must understand what we're facing."

Rhylan rounds the table and accesses a storage compartment above a computer center. He pulls out three of those communicator watches that Hawk, Lukas, and the others wear, as well as three data pads. He powers everything up and scans the watches with a data wand.

"Keeping the three of you in the loop will be easier if you're reachable. Hawk and Lukas got these for us from the Human Realm. They are a watch, a GPS tracker, a comms mic, a compass, an alarm, and a dozen other things. We're on a private network but can send requests to the quint and vise-versa in the case of an emergency."

He hands us each one and I fasten it to my wrist.

Rhylan taps the screen of his datapad a few times and then taps my watch with the wand. Then he repeats the process and taps Dune's.

"Okay, you're both online and activated. Now, you'll need chinos or fatigues with thigh pockets to hold your datapad. You'll pull it out to use pretty much every day all day. You can grab pants here at the castle or on your own. Your choice."

"Here is fine."

He nods. "All right. I'll upload those questions I mentioned, directions for how to get to the outfitting office, and you boys can take the next steps. I'll leave it to you to give Honor her communicator and datapad."

I clutch the security equipment in my hand, pleased with our progress already. "Now, can we revisit our idea about finding Amberloq warriors? We have a few ideas of where we might start."

Honor

I wake in the morning and scowl at the ornate ceiling above my bed. Why can't anything in my life be easy? When Lukas suggested we go to Amberloq Hall, I thought it was a fun idea. The four of us could get to know each other better, we'd learn about the Amberloq, my destiny, and maybe unravel a few of the mysteries…

Instead, Lukas and I fought, Amberloq Hall was in shambles, and the only opportunity to unravel mysteries denied us entry and left us with more questions.

It was frustrating, to say the least.

And then there was the other incident.

The goblin attack, me almost getting injected with something, and getting rescued by of all people... Keyla and her brother.

Rolling out of bed, I decide today is a new day. I'll thank Keyla properly, clear the air with the two of them, and apologize to Lukas, and clear the air with him.

Look at me making amends.

"Gah... when did I become such a disaster?"

"Hey, don't talk like that about my bestie." I turn and smile at my blonde and busty bestie bringing me a morning coffee.

Funny, in all the years I spent grooming her for this life, getting her off the street, and dragging her to every community center self-defense class I could sign us up for, I never pictured us changing places so dramatically.

Now she's the legendary phoenix, the beloved mate to four incredible and powerful men, and glowing with the radiance of carrying their little fireball.

And my life is a shitstorm.

"Hey, come in." I reach for the mug of morning sanity. "I need this more than I can say."

Calli's gaze locks on mine and she frowns. "Why do I get the feeling coffee isn't what you need most this morning? Or maybe not *who* you need most?"

I tip my mug, take a sip, and then set it on my dresser while I shuffle into the ensuite to pee. "No, I'm good. You'll never go wrong with a java fix."

"But maybe you were hoping for someone else to bring it to you? Maybe somebody with a sexy English accent, a chiseled jaw, and a six-pack that makes you panty-damp?"

"Maybe... but you're even better."

She snorts. "Yeah, practice saying that a few more times, and maybe I'll believe you."

That's the problem with best friends, even if you don't want to acknowledge what's going wrong with your life, they can see it and will call you on it.

"So, what's wrong?"

I finish washing my hands and come back and plunk on the bed. "What's right?"

I sit up, cross my legs, and reclaim my oversized mug of java. "You gotta give me somewhere to start. Is this Lukas trouble, Guardian of the Crown trouble, or Amberloq destiny trouble?"

"Yes."

"Oh dear. Coming at you from all fronts, is it?"

"Yes."

She fingers a chunk of her hair behind her ear and frowns. "All right, start with your sex life. It's obvi that you and Lukas have been highly charged and fighting a ton of sexual tension. Have you done the dance of twenty toes? Is he amazing in bed? Is he terrible in bed? Oh, gawd, don't tell me he's terrible in bed."

"From what I sampled, he's spectacular, but life took a turn and I don't think we'll be going anywhere near twenty toes again."

Her green eyes glitter as she waggles her eyebrows. "Why? Did he catch you getting down and dirty with your feathered fae? Was it a Princess sandwich?"

"No. Believe it or not, I don't jump into bed with someone because they're big and strong and sexy."

That makes her laugh. "The boys told me you and Lukas smelled like all kinds of orgasm the other day and that was like thirty-six hours after you met him. Then there was yesterday after the raid. You two were suspiciously late to regroup and my sources say you two were burning off adrenaline in the best possible way."

I choke on my dark roast. "Seriously? You and your men are gossiping about my orgasms?"

"No. They're more interested in Lukas's participation than yours. He's been with us for six months and has never carried the scent of a female on him. They're very excited for him putting himself out there. So, what did you do?"

I blink at her. "Me? That's judgy. Why point the finger at me?"

"Because it's your MO. You under commit and self-sabotage."

"Exqueeze me. I think that's a pot/kettle situation."

She grins. "Not anymore. Born again Calli is all-in. So, back to sex with Lukas. You knew him less than two days and were sexing... and?"

"Ugh... you're such a pain in the ass. I knew him less than two days on the living plane, yes, but we had a connection before that from when I was in my state of stasis. We spent weeks in a strangely intimate and vulnerable situation. I thought we built real bonds."

"I agree. Like I said, six months no sex. Two days with you, he's smiling and smelling like orgasms."

I close my eyes and scan the door to make sure it's closed tightly and our conversation is still our own.

Calli catches me checking the exit and frowns. "So it *is* about the winged warriors."

I take a long sip of coffee and try to settle my nerves. "My relationship with Tundra and Dune is all business at the moment. We've been working on getting to know each other and plan to start training together so we can learn to fight as a team."

"That's smart."

"Yeah, the next time someone comes at Creed or Keyla, I

want the Amberloq to be the ones fighting and risking their lives to save the royal couple, not you and Rhylan and the others."

Calli shrugs and adjusts the pillow behind her back. "Even if you have the Amberloq team of all teams, it wouldn't change anything about us jumping in. It's kinda what we do."

"Yeah, well you can't keep doing it. You're making a baby in there and my little god daughter needs to grow without you turning up the heat on her furnace."

She chuckles. "Kotah's researched every bit of the lore and says there's no way I'm hurting the baby. My shift is as natural as me being pregnant."

I wait for the impact of that to hit her, but she doesn't seem to find that statement nearly as crazy as I do. "Since when would you ever think the words natural and pregnant would be in a sentence you spoke?"

She shrugs. "I don't know what to tell you. At first, I wanted to puke—and it had nothing to do with morning sickness—but after a few weeks and now a few months, I'm used to the idea and am looking forward to it. Here, give me your hand."

I set my coffee on my nightstand and extend my hand to her. She closes her fingers around my wrist and places my palm against the round of her belly. I wait, closing my eyes to better detect if someone is wriggling around in there.

"I feel her... a little flutter... it's very rhythmic."

Calli giggles. "She has the hiccoughs. I think it's so cute, but what's even cuter is seeing how the boys get when they've got their hands on her and she does something. The four of them are out of their minds."

"That's sweet."

"It is. And Keyla and Creed have already decorated the nursery in the King's Tower and are waiting for their turn to babysit. Doc is building her a hand-carved cradle and Rhylan bought her the cutest dragon mobile you've ever seen."

The fact that Calli is more familiar with my brother and his mates than I am spears me with regret. "I told Creed we'd do better than our father and our aunt and yet here we are. He's on the other side of the castle starting his life with three people I barely know and I'm here wondering what the hell happened to my life."

Calli releases my hand and leans back against the headboard. "Why is it so hard for you to wrap your head around the fact that he is happy and loves his mates?"

"I think it's easier for you to accept them because you already knew Keyla and Dillan."

"Right, so I knew two and met two. How is that any different from where you're starting out?"

Well, when she says it that way, it's not.

"But Rhylan kept us prisoner."

"And if it hadn't been him, it would've been someone else. At least with him, he tried to keep you and Creed safe until things could change."

I take another long sip of coffee and wish it was spiked with amaretto like it would've been back in our apartment. "It sounds logical when you say it."

"Because it *is* logical. Rhylan was there for Creed during those years and gave him an outlet to stay sane."

I wince. "Please don't make me consider my brother using Rhylan for any kind of outlet."

She busts out laughing. "You realize that I have four male mates, right?"

"I am aware. Four incredibly hunky and fit mates, if I might add."

She grins. "You may, because hells yeah they are. Now, let's think about your situation. You're supposed to bond with the leaders of the biomes, but only two of the three showed up. Too bad, so sad."

"Well, it *is* too bad because the Amberloq force is decimated and so far only two warriors have shown up."

"Looking at it from a security force aspect, yes, no argument. That's terrible. I was talking about looking at it from the sexy mates angle."

I roll my eyes. "Most people have one mate and that's enough for them. My aunt had a husband and never had anything sexual with her warriors."

"Boring."

"Not boring."

"Is this what the trouble with Lukas is about? Is he giving you a hard time about the possibility of you mating with the Adonis angels out there?"

I shake my head. "No. That was an entirely different disaster."

"Okay, so, we're comfy, have coffee, and are alone. Go ahead and fill me in."

So, I do.

I tell Calli about Lukas's idea about exploring Amberloq Hall and then Dune calling him out about not being part of the 'we' team and how I kind of agreed. "He *is* a soldier loyal to another king who rules another realm. He has his own battles to wage. Amberloq Hall is a sanctum for Tundra and Dune. I didn't want them to lose that because I've got the hots for my boyfriend."

She makes a face. "What the hell, Ri—I mean Honor. Lukas is a logistics specialist with special ops and tactical training. He was whipping you and your boys into shape and was totally into you. And you sided with Dune and said he's odd man out? That's brutal."

I wince. "I didn't mean it like that. You know me, I'm not the best at expressing myself. What I was trying to say was yeah, I'm so thankful for everything he's done but I know he has other priorities. He's amazing, but this isn't his fight. He cares about me and my success but he's not Amberloq—he's just not."

Calli's mouth falls open. "Remember what Dumpster Doug used to say about 'buts'?"

I roll my eyes. "At the root of every but is an asshole. Hey, you're supposed to be on my side."

"Oh, I am. Don't kid yourself. Lukas is as good as they come and I'm watching you tank the beginnings of something amazing. Fix this. I don't care if it's an apology, or the best blowjob you've ever given, or an offer of making him an honorary Amberloq. You're going to tell him your lead vault brain-trap killed off brain cells and you need a mulligan on that convo."

"But what about Dune and Tundra? Is it fair to them if my attention is divided? Maybe I should focus on Amberloq stuff. Valorous chose her lover over what she needed to do and everyone died."

"Stop comparing yourself to a woman who left you unprepared. You respected your father, yes?"

"Yeah, he was an amazing leader and Dornte loved him because he was fair and believed in his people. Creed is just like him. All we need to do is keep him safe long enough to set things right."

"And you don't think Lukas is a huge asset for that? He's been running Hawk's security squad for more than a decade. He's been dealing with assassination attempts, corporate espionage, and billionaire crazies longer than anyone you know. It seems to me if you want your Amberloq squad to have the best chance at success, he's exactly the man you need on the team."

I think about that and of course, she's right.

"Dammit. This is going to suck."

"Yep."

"And I suppose I should apologize right away?"

"Yep."

Man, I'm glad to have Calli in my life—my real life—even though her living across the corridor is only temporary. "Hey, what are you doing here, anyway? I thought you were heading back through the gate to be the queen of the realm with Kotah."

"We were but then last night happened."

I wave that away. "I told you I'm fine. I have to eat crow and thank Keyla for the rescue, but other than that, no harm done."

Calli shrugs and sits up, finishing her coffee. "And that's awesome, but after what happened last night... I wanted to stay and check on you, and, of course, Hawk wanted to stay and check on Lukas."

I swallow. "Lukas? What happened to Lukas?"

Calli makes a face and my insides knot. "I didn't mention it last night because of what happened to you, and it was late, and things were a bit up in the air. Rhylan located Hawk's asshole half-brother and they went out to grab him up."

"Did they get him?"

She nods. "Jaxx and Rhylan chased him down, yeah, but in the scuffle, there was a shooting—"

"Lukas was *shot?*" A rush of adrenaline hits and I have to brace myself against the headboard to fight the wave of dizziness. She takes my mug before I drop it and I breathe through the spinning of the world. "Is he all right?"

"I expect he's fine by now. All of us carry a vial of my phoenix tears to combat fatal injury. Hawk was right there when he fell to the pavement, so he was able to administer them right away."

The thought of Lukas falling to the pavement shot and bleeding cleaves me in two.

No one even told me.

Did he tell them not to? Is he so angry with me that he didn't want me to know... or be with him?

The strain between us is a physical ache in my chest. I need to get to him and fix this. I need to make things right between us.

I swipe at the hot tears on my cheeks and turn toward Calli. "Where is he?"

CHAPTER NINETEEN

Lukas

*W*aking up in the chair beside Shadow's bedside, I stretch my neck and frown at the purple-haired elf lying motionless in the bed. Calli's tears should've done their healing work by now. Even if he wasn't a hundred percent, he should be awake.

Unless he's suffered a brain injury.

Even then. Jaxx had more obvious head trauma than him and he had woken up by now.

There must be something else going on.

I wrench myself out of the chair and press my hands on both sides of Shadow's cheeks. Closing my eyes, I probe what I can to see if there's anything magical going on. It's a long shot, but after working with Honor and talking to Creed about working on his curse, I thought maybe.

There isn't though.

No tampering. Nothing for me to do to help.

"Get better, my friend. After everything that's gone down, I was hoping to put your counseling services to use. Yes, fine, I admit I crossed a line with Honor, but I don't think it was a decision so much as a foregone conclusion. She and I have a connection beyond two isolated adults. Maybe as I untangled the Blood Witches hold on her, I tangled myself. Or maybe it's fate or destiny or just good old-fashioned head over heels love."

At least on my side.

After last night, I honestly don't know where I stand with her. So, yeah, talking it out with the counselor would be nice.

If he wasn't in a coma.

I straighten, grip my shoulder pinching the muscle that locked up tight, and wonder if the kink will work itself out or if I'll need a massage.

Another comfort of privilege I got used to while working with Hawk for a decade. How can a man who seems so steely hard have habits that make me feel soft as a pansy's petals?

Speak of the devil.

The soft knock on the door trim has me finishing my stretching as I join him in the hall.

I raise my arm and meet my closest friend's gaze. "Thanks for the save last night."

He clasps my palm and pulls me against his chest for a back-slap hug. "You're way ahead of me in the life-saving moments, but if you don't mind, I'd rather you not even things out."

I chuckle and ease back. "I'll try to keep that in mind. Dying is overrated anyway."

"Definitely."

The two of us fall quiet for a moment and then my instincts kick in and the hair on the back of my neck stands on end. "What? Did Hunter escape?"

He shakes his head. "No. Rhylan's got him locked up tight and is letting him stew. I told him you'd want to be there for the interrogation."

"Fuck, yeah, I do."

He locks me in a stare, the muscle in his jaw twitching.

That's a tell for him. There's something that needs saying and he doesn't want to say it wrong.

"Just spit it out. Who and what?"

"Honor. Last night when we were out, she was attacked by goblins on the castle grounds. She sent Dune and Tundra back to the suite and—"

"She was alone?"

"She was."

"Is she all right?"

"She is. Calli is with her…" Hawk's words trail off in the distance as I rush through the halls of the King's Tower guest area toward the exit.

My fingers are snapping with magic as my emotions run wild. Fuck. I need to get a hold of that before I lose control and short out the castle's power.

Honor was attacked.

She was *alone* and attacked.

Did she fight off the goblins? I can't imagine that. She was exhausted and emotionally drained after the memorial… and I'm sure our fight didn't help.

Is that why she was on the grounds alone at night?

Did me leaving in a huff put her in the crosshairs of… Fuck. Questions spin in my mind, multiplying with every thundering footstep.

"Lukas? Is everything—"

"Fine," I say, cutting off Doc's concern as I race past the great room in Creed's suite. I don't know that everything is fine. I hope it is.

I need for it to be.

As I make it to the grand entrance the heavy door flies open and Honor is racing through.

My breath locks in my chest as I take inventory of her. Is she hurt? Other than the tears in her eyes and the fact that she raced through the entire castle in her silky baby doll, all seems right with her.

She doesn't stop when she sees me.

She beelines straight at me and our bodies collide. I stagger back a few steps to catch her as she wraps her arms around my neck and her legs around my hips.

Her mouth on mine is the sweetest torture.

She tastes of coffee and salty tears. I sweep my tongue into her mouth, chasing the flavor.

Possession and fear roar through me in heavy doses. She could've been killed. She could've been taken from me because a hit to my ego sent me storming off.

Anger and lust roar through me next. I need to hold her and reassure myself she's all right but we're standing in the center of her brother's entranceway making out with people staring at us.

I ease back from the kiss, get her feet back onto the floor, and press my forehead to hers. "I'm sorry."

She shakes her head and pegs me with those passionate purple eyes of hers. "No. *I'm* sorry. I was stupid and insensitive."

"You were tired and emotionally drained."

"It's no excuse. If you died with hurt feelings and angry at me, I would never have gotten over it."

I pull her against my chest and run my hand through her long, silver hair. "I didn't die so there's nothing to get over."

"So, we can fix it?"

"There's nothing to fix."

Calli grins wide from inside the front door and winks to someone over my shoulder. With Honor still in my arms, I swivel to see who's there.

Not that I need to.

"Care to let us in on the secret?" I ask Hawk. "What are you two up to?"

Hawk holds up his hands. "Not a thing. We weren't meddling and we certainly weren't stirring either of you up to illustrate how short life is and how meaningless it would be without the person you love."

"Absolutely not," Calli says. "But if we were interfering it would only be because we know you both so well and we see what you two can be together."

I roll my eyes. "You matchmaking again, Calli?"

She grins. "You told me in the raft that day on the river that you wanted to find a quint of your own. And, if I remember correctly, I said that if I had any friends I liked enough to set you up with, I totally would."

I laugh. "My point was that it would serve you guys right to be on the outside of a sex-obsessed fivesome and constantly be walking in on inappropriate situations and lewd and lust-filled moments."

Hawk walks around me to collect Calli against his side. "Bring it on, magic man. We can out-do your inappropriate coitus interruptus any day of the week."

Honor chuckles. "How did this become a contest?"

Calli laughs. "Oh, there's no contest. There's nothing we could walk in on that would put my guys off. They love inappropriate so we've already won."

"You'll have to hold off on your fivesome competition," Honor says. "Lukas and I are only two and the jury is still out whether or not Dune and Tundra will rip each other to shreds in the coming weeks."

Calli flashes a look and laughs. "Oh, I think they'll survive. You know how we were talking about walking in on inappropriate situations?"

"Yeah."

"Well, when Keyla sent word that you'd been attacked, I rushed across the hall to tell your two feathered warriors and they were going at it hard and polishing the countertop in your kitchen."

Honor blinks. "What? Seriously?"

"Oh, yeah. I didn't stick around long…"

"However tempted," Hawk says, chuckling.

Calli looks up and shrugs. "I'm a voyeur, sue me, and hello, no one with eyes would blame me if I stuck around for a few extra seconds…"

"Because you did."

Calli grins, unrepentant. "Because those boys are chiseled and fine and quite well-conditioned."

I blink and turn to Honor. "Did you know they've been crossing swords?"

"No. Then again, we only met them three days ago and they spent the past two years together." She looks at Calli and shakes her head. "You're sure? Dune and Tundra? I thought they hated each other."

"Lots of energy in hate sex," Hawk says.

Calli waggles her blonde brows. "And the heat they were throwing off as they went at it could rival my phoenix flame any day."

Out of nowhere, my mind lights up with erotic images of the two of them going at it and my blood rushes straight to my cock. I swallow and turn to look at Honor. "That's not helpful in mixed company."

She blushes and glances down to the front of my pants. It's obvious I've got a hard-on and what makes it worse is how her eyes light up as she's looking me over. "Sorry. I forgot you're on my wavelength."

The second round of images light off and in this fantasy series, I'm naked and joining the other two.

I cough and adjust my stance. "Okay, you need to stop. You're killing me here."

Honor shrugs. "Not my fault. You gave me the idea. And you told Calli you needed your own quint. I can't help it if I have powerful mind energy. I'm a mind guardian fae, after all."

No amount of shifting my feet will help me now. I give up

on propriety, reach down my fatigues, and adjust things. "If you two will excuse us. There are a few things we need to take care of rather urgently."

Calli giggles. "We'll walk with you... assuming you can make it that far without blue balls taking you out."

"We can," Honor says, and then she looks at me. "Can't we?"

I swallow. "If we leave right now and you don't have any erotic big ideas between here and there."

"I'll try to be good. Until we're alone, I'll focus on what we found at Amberloq Hall, and then you can help me plan how to unravel the mystery of a DNA scanner in the library."

Tundra

When Dune and I return from our workout and speaking with Rhylan, we're both in good spirits and feeling like we accomplished something. I place my hand on the security scanner beside the door to Honor's suite and it unlocks for me without issue.

Access is granted and even though it is a small thing, it means a lot to me. It means I belong here.

We belong here.

"These watches are slecking cool," Dune says, holding his wrist up and adjusting dials as he walks into the suite. "It's got GPS and a compass and now that we've been added into the system, we can track the location of the others wearing them."

"And once Honor has hers on, we'll be able to track her if anything happens."

"As long as she doesn't take it off or if it's not taken off her." Dune frowns and I suspect he's thinking about last night.

If he hadn't started the argument with Lukas, he likely would have been with her when she went to visit her brother.

Honor was put at risk because she was hurt and wanted time alone.

She almost lost her life because of it.

And where were we?

Serving one another instead of her.

I set the datapads down on the coffee table and check my new tactical watch. "Lukas possesses expertise in military training and technology from his world. Things that can be added to our knowledge and make us stronger. Perhaps we were rash in dismissing his possible contribution to our team."

Dune perches his ass on the arm of the couch and sighs. "I hate being the one who made Honor so sad. As much as I don't want to share her with him because he isn't part of our destiny, I suppose, it isn't my call."

"No. It's not." Honor strides through the door behind us wearing nothing but her silky lingerie.

Lukas follows close behind and closes the door.

"It took both of us almost dying last night to remember that *I* am the Guardian of the Crown, and you are here to support me."

I drop my chin. "Of course, milady. Apologies."

Dune nods. "I apologize as well, Princess."

"Your apologies are accepted." She stops beside the coffee table, the silk of her skimpy pajamas shimmering in the light. "Lukas adds to my life both personally and strategically and is not going anywhere. The fact that he was raised in the Human Realm and is not an Amberloq soldier adds to our strength, it doesn't diminish it."

I meet Lukas's gaze and nod. "We were just discussing that very thing. Rhylan set us up with these watches and taught us a little about the security infrastructure you are helping him build. It is impressive."

Lukas offers us a tight nod. "The way I look at it, the three of you are bound and determined to keep Creed and the realm safe. Honor and I are bound as well and I am equally deter-mined to keep her safe. The two objectives overlap, but with me here, there will always be someone who can put her first."

Dune frowns. "And what does that mean for us... beyond the soldiering, I mean."

Honor smiles. "Honestly, new light was shed on that just this morning. I didn't know the two of you have a sexual relation-ship. Now that I do, I'm intrigued."

I straighten, my mind spinning.

Dune launches to his feet. "I don't know what you think you know, Princess, but—"

"Relax boys," Lukas says, holding up his palms. "You're busted. Accept it. Last night when Honor was attacked, Calli rushed in here to tell the two of you. She got an eyeful. There's no denying it."

I rub a hand over my face. "Then you also know how badly we failed you. While you were being stalked and attacked, we were... distracted."

Honor chuckles. "It's fine. I asked you two to return to the suite. You getting distracted on your own time is perfectly fine. Better than fine, actually."

"Why? What do you mean?" I ask.

She shrugs. "I've been struggling with the conflict of what the four of us might be. But the conflict was all I could see: the conflict between Dune and Lukas, the conflict between the two of you, the conflict between me wanting Lukas to remain in my life and in my bed and what that would mean to our joining."

"And how does Tundra and I taking out our frustrations together help you?" Dune asks.

"Let me show you."

My mind floods with erotic images of the four of us. Lukas sliding her silky bottoms off while Dune and I hold her knees open so he can feast on her cream.

Then the four of us on the balcony under the light of the

moon, laying her out on the patio cushions. I'm buried deep inside her and pumping while she's got her hands wrapped around Dune's and Lukas's cock.

Then her on her knees sucking on Lukas's cock while Dune thrusts into her and I thrust into him.

Dune and Lukas both groan and I realize she's sharing these scenarios with all three of us.

"Who here is throwing wood like a horny lumberjack?" Lukas asks, his voice husky.

Dune and I both raise our hands. The time for discretion is over. Our princess is looking for us being forthright and real.

"And how do you feel about this scenario, Lukas?" I think I know the answer based on the pressure being exerted on the zipper of his pants but would like to hear him say it.

Lukas swallows. "I try not to define things. I've seen the devastation wars and military conflict brings. I tend to be more of a live-and-let-live sort of guy. Life's too short to be who you're not and judge others for being who they are."

Honor chuckles. "That's very bohemian of you."

He shrugs. "He asked. I answered."

She sobers, looking far less amused. "So, it truly doesn't bother you that I'm bound to them and want to share my body with other men?"

Lukas shrugs. "If it's your custom and what you believe is your destiny, what good is it for me to be bothered? When Calli was bonded with the quint, there was no question. When Keyla bonded with your brother, it was a bit messier because Doc and Rhy were add-ins. It wasn't cut and dry, but it didn't make them any less important."

"No. You wouldn't be any less important. The connection we have is equally important but different."

He shrugs and smiles. "So, if you're not tossing me to the side, I'm game. If you were saying they stay and I go—yeah, I'd be bothered. Very bothered."

Honor's entire body radiates happiness. Her wings release and flutter behind her. "Good answer."

The implications of this conversation are still stirring my arousal. Between Honor's sex images and Lukas locking things down, it sounds like this might happen.

Maybe even right now.

"It sounds like you thought this through," I say.

Lukas nods. "However it happened—whether it was a side effect of the curse or my presence within her or nature's design, Honor and I are connected. I'm not about to walk away simply because she's destined for more. Like Dune said about his nomadic community, everyone has strengths and can contribute to the whole."

I agree. "As far as I am concerned, you are a strong soldier, an asset to our cause, and bound to Princess Honor in your own way. You are welcome. I am sorry I ever made you feel otherwise."

Dune rolls his eyes. "Fine. You being human doesn't seem as bad as I thought. If Honor is choosing to add Tundra and me into her personal life, I won't object to you being there too."

Honor grins. "Glad we all agree and I think to solidify that, we should get naked—like right now."

"Thank fuck." Lukas wraps his arm around Honor and scoops her bare feet off the ground. Lifting her to his chest, he starts for the bedroom. "Time to get our female naked, boys."

CHAPTER TWENTY

Lukas

My cock is thick and pulsing, hungry to be swallowed inside Honor's heat. That will have to wait. This is the first time for the four of us and I want to make sure we're all on the same page.

I lay her out on the top of the bed in my room and man, she sucks the breath from my lungs. With her long, silver hair fanned out on the pillow beneath her, she looks like a living angel.

I force myself to look away and address Dune and Tundra. "I say we start with Honor's erotic slideshow and go from there. That way, we're focused on her, and will have a chance to get comfortable with one another."

Tundra unstraps the side fasteners of his vest and bares the sculpted abs of his chest. His gaze is locked on Honor laid out like a goddess, his expression reverent. "Our lady has needs. It is our duty to fulfill them."

Dune's vest is already off and he's shoving his pants to the floor. The guy is as sculpted and fit as Tundra and I can see why Calli was so enraptured while watching them together.

"First comes the appetizer. Then the main course." Dune tilts his head toward the bed. "I believe you had the starring role in the first movie, soldier. You're up."

"Understatement of the century." I waggle my brows, strip off my shirt, and face the end of the bed while I shuck off my pants.

As I climb onto the bed, Honor gazes down the length of her body at me. "You prowl like a predator about to devour his prey."

I grin and lower my mouth, nipping the inside of her knee. "Oh, you are definitely about to be devoured."

I settle in below the Mason Dixon Line and sit back on my knees. "Boys, I believe you're supposed to be at her sides and holding her open."

Honor's cheeks are a lovely shade of embarrassment and I have to chuckle. "This is your doing. Are you having second thoughts?"

"No. It's just… a little new."

I wait until Dune settles in on one side and Tundra on the other. "How about you introduce yourselves properly gentlemen?"

Tundra leans in to claim Honor's mouth and smiles. "I have a rule about first kisses, Princess. I never start anywhere but right here. So, hello, and thank you for inviting us into your bed."

He slides his hand along her jaw and under her hair, lifting her lips to his. The meeting of their mouths is gentle and sweet and I see how much appreciation our iceman holds for her.

When he pulls back, he kisses her once, twice more before he eases back. "That was lovely."

Honor nods. "It was."

All eyes shift to Dune and for the first time, his cocky air falls away and he offers her a genuine look at the man beneath the bravado. "I'm honored to be your general, Princess. I promise you, I will do my best to make you proud to have me at your side."

He brushes his finger over her lips and breaks the seal of her mouth. She welcomes the invasion of his finger, suckling and swirling her tongue over it before nipping hard.

He stiffens and then laughs. "Oh, our Lady Thornebane is a biter."

"Guilty," she giggles.

"So be prepared," I say.

Dune groans. "I will take any punishment you choose to give me, but thanks for the warning."

She lifts her head to look at me kneeling at the crux of her body and lifts her knees. "I believe we have a fantasy to act out. Generals, if you will."

Tundra and Dune snuggle against her sides and hook their arms under her knees spreading her wide for my viewing pleasure. I swallow, taking in the glistening of her folds and the way the guys are pinning her open for me. With her legs up, I've now got an up and personal view of Dune and Tundra's junk and how much they're enjoying this.

"Fuck, this is insanely hot," I say, my cock thrumming with a pulse of its own.

Tundra leans in and shows Honor some love, suckling on her nipple and drawing his tongue across her heated skin.

Dune makes his way down her sternum, licking the ink of the lineage tattoo that runs from her shoulder, over the mound of her breast, and to the jut of her hip bone.

Honor's eyes roll closed as she arches her chest into the air. "I like insanely hot."

Dune catches me watching and tilts his head. "Don't you have a job to do, soldier?"

The jab doesn't hold any of his usual cutting edge, so I take it as it was meant. As an invitation to get this party started. I can't say I'm a huge fan of the guy but if he's willing to try, I will do the same.

Sliding down onto my belly, I make myself comfortable. Drawing my tongue up the sensitive flesh of her inner thigh brings forward a rush of goosebumps.

Glancing up, I watch as her nipples become even harder. I smile, dropping my head to give her a proper greeting. As I claim her core and drag my tongue through the rush of moisture that meets me there, my mind misfires and my cells ignite.

She groans and grinds against my kiss with the same energy and need for more.

She tastes like ambrosia—fucking food of the gods.

With my tongue flicking and fluttering over her folds, I make it clear that this is where I'm meant to be. Amberloq or not, she belongs to me as much as I belong to her. She's incredible.

Addictive.

The three of us play a few minutes more before she's groaning. "Please. I'm wet and weeping and aching for some attention."

I laugh against her core. "Aren't you getting enough attention with three of us tending to you, Princess? My, goodness, you are a greedy girl."

Tundra nips the peak of her nipple, and she gasps.

As a fresh rush of cream hits my tongue, I swallow and dive in to lap it up. "Fuck, you are so wet... and beautifully bare."

I nuzzle against the satin of her pale, porcelain skin. Her body is barer than shaving or waxing could ever accomplish. This is a faery thing.

"Oh, yes," she gasps.

"You like what Lukas is doing?" Tundra asks, his voice a seductive caress.

"Yes, but I need more."

"Do you want to come against his mouth?"

"Yes."

Fuck yes. I want that too. Gripping the globes of her ass, I lift her hips against my mouth and eat her without apology. There's nothing gentlemanly about the way I go at her. It's carnal and primal.

"Yes," she whispers, thrusting against my mouth.

I love a woman who knows what she wants.

The way she rocks against the pressure of my mouth while Dune and Tundra play with her tits... it's so erotic. "Let's make her come hard, boys," I say.

She groans. "So hard."

Releasing her ass, I shift my grip and slide my thumb through the moisture surrounding her clit.

Her legs quiver against the sides of my head. She's close. The erotic sounds of her panting breath and her little feminine groans are so fucking gratifying.

Flicking my tongue around and then into her pussy, I have my fun and drive her wild. Tundra and Dune are busy doing their part to blow her mind, and if I'm reading her body language right, we're doing a good job.

Increasing the pressure of my thumb makes her groan and I smile and increase it some more. Faster. Rougher. When her breath quickens, I think about slowing down a bit and making her ride it out for a while, but honestly, she's been through enough torture.

This is all about Honor gratification.

Her legs start to tremble a moment before she stills and the muscles of her pussy start to clench and tighten in greedy pulls around my tongue.

"Yes!" she hisses, grinding against my mouth like a wild woman. As her orgasm takes her, I tongue-fuck her like a champion and a fresh rush of cream is my reward.

Damn, she tastes good... like crazy good.

As the greedy pulses begin to slow, I let her catch her breath and the guys release her legs so she can stretch out and ride out her afterglow.

"A good start?" I ask.

"A great start. Thank you."

"What would you like next?" Tundra asks.

Her grin is much too sexy. "I think I got first pick."

Dune chuckles. "You're in luck. It's lady's choice."

Based on the smile that earns us, I think that was the right answer. She bites her bottom lip and seems to think about that. "Honestly, I need to be filled or my ovaries might explode. Tundra will you make love to me? And then I want to suck off Dune and toss Lukas."

The three of us do a quick check-in and nod.

After a bit of scrambling on the bed, Tundra and I switch places, Dune and I move up the bed so we can watch and establish a slow stroke on ourselves.

I don't put too much into touching myself. I'm ready to blow now and the moment Tundra pushes inside her, I swear I'm going to lose control.

Doesn't matter. This is the beginning of what's to come and after watching the others form their bonds, I know I'm in for one helluva ride.

Honor

My mind is spinning. There's so much I want to try, to feel, to do. I want to stay like this forever. Who needs to eat? The four of us can be naked and greedy and orgasm and let life carry on without us.

Tundra lowers his hips between my legs, notches his swollen crown at my entrance, and looks up at me. "I am honored to be your lover. You have my word I shall live my life to fulfill your needs in and out of the bedroom."

"Thank you, Tundra. I promise the same. We need to be more than lovers. We need to be partners and fellow warriors. This is the beginning of something great, I feel it."

Speaking of feeling it.

Tundra presses forward, the penetration deep, the wet glide and slide sinfully delicious. "Oh, my, you feel good in there. I needed this."

He pauses while our bodies adjust. "I'm glad you think so. And I agree, by the way.

He begins a slow and seductive rock of his hips and I lay back to absorb the pleasure.

Tundra is a beautiful warrior, his body chiseled and exquisite. I've had lovers—both here before the war and as Riley in the human world—but I have a feeling these men will surpass them all.

He's hard and thick and when his hips thrust all the way inside me, he hits something delicious.

A zing of pleasure makes me gasp with each full penetration.

"Gawd, that's so good," I gasp. My voice is breathless and pitchy. Not the type of sound a warrior queen should make but I don't care. Another orgasm is building inside me, and my insides are tightening with the promise of detonation.

Reaching above his head, I gently grip his horns. "I've heard the horns of the Elbirfae are an erogenous zone, like the spinal ridges where my wings eject.

Tundra's eyes roll back, and he swallows. "You heard right. That feels incredible... but if you want me to last, you shouldn't stroke my horns too much. I don't want you to be disappointed."

I grin and lower my hands to grip his muscled shoulders. "For now, I want more sexing. I'll come back to the horns again soon."

He lowers his head and claims my mouth.

The *slap-slap-slap* of flesh hitting flesh is primal and I'm so thankful I chose to focus on him solo for our first encounter. It allows me the chance to be present in the moment.

"He's holding back," Dune says. "Are you ready for more, Princess?"

More? There's more? "Yes. Give me everything."

He bites his bottom lip as he does sometimes and then something shifts inside me. It's subtle at first and then the nerve endings in my body tingle to full awareness. A chill snaps in my core.

"Oh," I gasp, arching into the sensation.

Dune chuckles, brushing his fingers over the glistening mounds of my breasts.

My nipples tighten as an icy tingle takes hold inside of me and my inner muscles start to convulse.

I can't think. The crispness of cool at the same time he's pumping inside me...

My mind is spinning.

This orgasm shatters me, and I buck beneath him as my body convulses in glorious waves. Tundra shows me no mercy, his breathy grunts getting louder until his hips lock and he arches back.

I watch his expression as he climaxes and it's a painful beauty. When he stills, I smile and revel in the aftershocks of my release, my inner muscles pulsing and gripping his cock.

And what a magnificent cock it is.

As the last of his thrusts subsides, he drops to his elbows and we lay body to body.

I pant, trying to catch my breath. "What was that you did inside me? I've never felt anything like it."

He winks and brushes his lips over mine. "Elbirfae males have a barb we can release from our crown. It extends our reach and taps into a female's nerve center. It's quite effective for enhancing pleasure."

I chuckle, kissing him back. "Quite effective indeed. Thank you."

When my breathing returns to normal, I wink at Dune and smile. "Don't think I've forgotten you."

He shakes his head and flashes me one of his cocky grins. "How could you? No. I know you just saved the best until last."

CHAPTER TWENTY-ONE

Honor

$\mathcal{A}$fter a glorious afternoon of orgasms and getting to know the guys better, the four of us visit Amberloq Hall to see if we can access whatever mystery we're missing in the library. I have no doubt Lukas can figure it out—he's a strategic guy plus he has magic on his side.

"Is there a spell you can cast to see the unseen or to find the hidden path that will show us what we missed yesterday?"

He smiles at me as we enter the iron gate. "Very good, Princess. That's almost exactly right."

The compliment warms me, and I pat myself on the back. Though I don't know anything about mage magic, other than he doesn't like it when I equate him to being a witch or wizard, I'm certain he is quite good at it.

After all, he undid the binds of the Blood Witch and she was the biggest, baddest witch bitch in our realm.

The four of us climb the front steps of the once-grand headquarters of my warrior sect and it pains me as much today as it did yesterday—maybe more.

The ruins of what was once great.

Tundra squeezes my shoulder and casts me a soft smile. "We will rebuild. You'll see. With you at the helm and the three of us working at your side, we will repopulate our numbers and become the force we once were."

I sigh. "It's such a shame that we're in this situation. Valorous never should have separated from my father. She should've accepted her warriors and fought to keep my parents safe and our quadrant on track."

Lukas opens the door for us and turns on the lights. "You'll learn from her mistakes. Take what she did right with her warriors and amend her shortcomings in the areas where she fell short. You've got this."

"We've got this," I say, taking in the shambles I've inherited. "With a rebel force actively working to stop us, we need to pull up our socks and get ready for the battles ahead."

"Exactly right," Creed says, coming through the door behind us. He steps aside to allow Keyla to enter first and then Calli and her four warriors follow carrying boxes and bins of supplies.

"We'll be ready. I've thought a lot about where our predecessors went wrong, and we won't make the same mistakes."

"No, we won't," Keyla says, bathing my brother in an adoring gaze. "We have two realms of knowledge and all the support we could ever need to make things right for Dornte and the entire Fae Realm."

"Hells, yeah, you do," Calli says.

I look at the seven of them and smile. "What are you guys doing here? I thought you were headed back to Pennsylvania."

"Not before we check out your new digs." Calli steps deeper into the grand entrance and scrunches her nose. "You've got a real fixer-upper on your hands here, chickie. Almost as bad as our apartment when we first moved in."

I snort. "Nothing is as bad as our apartment when we first moved in."

Her grin splits wide. "The point is, we whipped that place into shape, and we'll do the same here. A little birdie told us that there was work to do, so here we are."

She winks at Dune and he shrugs. "When everyone contributes, it strengthens the whole."

"And we brought reinforcements," Keyla says, opening the door wider to welcome a dozen of the castle brownies.

I've always known brownies worked behind the scenes to keep the castle running, but I've rarely caught sight of them. Fae brownies are the size of toddlers with long ears pointing out the sides of their heads and wide, round eyes.

They love to work hard and live to serve, but I've never known them to interact with the members of our castle.

Keyla sets a hand on one of the male's backs and smiles. "When I mentioned to Meri that we have a massive cleaning and organizing job to do, he was excited to tell the others and volunteer to help."

The brownie grins up at her and says something in a language I don't understand.

"He'd like to know if there will be people moving in to live here once again. He will ensure you have the staff you need."

"That's the plan, yes, but for now, there will only be us." I open my hands and wave them in. "Thank you. I'm touched and so appreciative. Welcome."

The little army of cleaners move in and Brant, Hawk, and Jaxx set the boxes of supplies down by the open staircase.

Calli watches them dig in and shuffle off and giggles. "No dust will settle on them."

Keyla shakes her head. "No. They are wonderful. And as an FYI, they love gummy bears and little gemstones the best as thank you gifts."

Thank you, gifts? In all the years, I never once thought to leave gifts for the brownies.

Creed seems to follow my train of thought and speaks

directly into my mind. *I'm telling you, Honor, she's truly spectacular.*

As the crowd disperses and people start to look around, I draw a deep breath and suck it up. Making my way over to my brother and his wife, I do what I should've done days ago.

"I apologize to you both. I was on my way to say this when I was attacked last night, so it didn't get said, but it's true. I haven't been fair to either of you. Your love is none of my business, but if it were, I'd say that I realize you're more than you appear. Yes, you're young and kind and have a fresh outlook on things, but you're also brave and loyal and willing to fight for the people around you, whether they deserve it or not."

Keyla's warm, brown gaze softens. "You've never stopped deserving it, Honor. Even if you weren't Creed's sister or Calli's best friend, you are a woman who suffered a trauma and needed a moment to recalibrate. I don't blame you for that."

"Neither do I," Creed says.

Keyla tucks a loose strand of hair behind her ear and smiles. "When my brother came back to our palace six months ago, I was angry. He left me alone to fend for myself in a hostile, toxic world. He was happy, had four mates who adored him, and I felt forgotten. I made his life more difficult than it needed to be and he called me out on it. That was my frustration and pain coming out and wasn't who I truly was—nor is it you."

I swallow. "Yeah, that pretty much nails what I was going to say."

Creed chuckles and hugs me. "I'm so glad to have you back. You'll never know how much it hurt me to know you were out there fighting Laryssa on your own. I'm so sorry I couldn't be more help."

I hug him back, the ache of regret and frustration tainting his mental energy. "It's over. Eyes on the horizon. We've got a future to start navigating."

"Which starts right now," Lukas says, holding his hand out

for me to join him. "I think I've got your library mystery figured out. Let's give it a try."

He squeezes my hand as he leads me back into the library where Dune, Tundra, Calli, and Hawk are waiting. "I need you to set things in motion. Go ahead. Do your thing."

Stepping up to the bookshelf, I eye up the glossy, mirrored surface staring back at me. "Be kind today. Open Sesame."

When I press my hand on the DNA scanner, I hold my breath for a couple of heartbeats until the soft *click* tells me we're in business.

"So, we think that means something unlocked."

Lukas extends his arms and his hands glow blue, swallowed by an aura of magic. His lips move but whatever he's saying is too quiet to be heard.

As he moves slowly across the bookshelf, holding his hands forward, I try not to be impatient. It's difficult. I don't want things to lock up again and time us out.

Although, that took quite a long time yesterday.

"Here," he points to a marble bust sitting on one of the shelves. "The release is connected to something here but I think it should be you who finds it. If it's designed to only allow the female Thornebane to access, I don't want to get us locked out."

"My thoughts exactly." I move over to where Lukas indicated and feel around the statue. "Anyone know who this is I'm groping?"

Creed comes over and frowns. "No idea."

Calli smiles. "Something for our scholars to research. I'm sure Kotah and Doc will love to figure that one out."

Keyla nods. "Doc wanted to be here, but he didn't want to leave Shadow. He's hoping today is the day he'll regain consciousness."

"I hope so too." Something inside of me aches for Shadow to wake up. Maybe it's the trauma of being there when he was hurt or understanding too well what it's like to be trapped in a coma or something else entirely.

Whatever it is, Shadow is dominantly on my mind.

I grip the jaw of the man's face and tip the statue back. Surprisingly, the base stays on the shelf, and only his head tips back. "Bingo. We have a winner."

Flicking the switch hidden within, I wait to see what happens next.

A louder *click* sounds and Dune looks to his left. "That was definitely here."

I hurry over to where he's pointing to one of the panels of the wall and smile. "This is the same as our private panels in our suites. I've got this."

I press on the panel and shift it out of the way. Instead of a safe, like in my closet, this private panel exposes a dark opening into a chamber beyond. Stale air rushes out and tingles in my sinuses. Whatever's inside here hasn't been looked at in decades.

"Go ahead Princess," Dune says beside me. "This is what you've been building toward your whole life."

"He's right," Tundra says. "This is it."

I look back and see the excited smiles on the faces of family and friends. I'm so incredibly thankful for all the help they've given me over the past week.

And, as much as I want them to join me on the next part of the adventure, my instincts tell me I am meant to travel this part of the journey alone.

A shiver of energy races up my spine and my fingers start to tingle. I draw in a breath and take a step closer to the dark entrance to the chamber.

"You've got this," Lukas says.

"Yeah, I do." I step through the opening, trailing my fingers along the smooth, pale stone.

I've got this.

Shadow

The dreams have stopped. The tingling and numbness have subsided. Now if I could only get rid of this buzzing in my skull. Thankfully, the lights are off, so it's dark and not making matters worse.

I raise my hands to touch the bandages on my head.

What happened?

I close my eyes and sift through the wooly fog blanketing my mind. The last thing I remember is being in the truck on the way to the Dornte memorial... Lukas swerved the truck into oncoming traffic... someone shot a missile at us? Yes. Someone shot a missile at us.

The scene unfolds in choppy detail.

The memory makes my heart race and the monitors start beeping wildly. I reach down and pull the leads off my chest and free my fingers. Now the alarms are sounding and it's even worse than the beeping.

"Shadow, welcome back, my friend," Doc says to my right. "How are you feeling?"

"I shall do." There is not much more to be said because wildlings can smell the scent of a lie. "I admit, I am thankful to be awake even with the headache."

There. That was all true.

"What happened? Is everyone all right?"

The alarms stop screaming and I let out a breath, thankful for the silence.

"Everyone is well. We caught one of the street bandits as well as Hawk's half-brother. Rhylan and Lukas are letting them stew and will be interrogating them soon. We'll know more about what the attack was about in the next few days."

"What about the memorial?"

"It happened. Everyone was a little war-torn, but I was told the citizens were happy Creed and Honor were alive to commemorate their parents."

"You weren't there?"

"No. I stayed with you and brought you back to the castle clinic. You were the worst off."

Lucky me.

"You hit your head but even so, I've been worried. You didn't come around as quickly as I expected. Now that you're awake, maybe we can figure out why."

The idea of lying here for tests doesn't appeal.

"There is no need to worry. I regret you missed the memorial because of me though. My apologies."

Doc chuckles, removing the bandages wrapped around my head. "There's no need to apologize. I'm a field medic and doctor first and always. Creed, Keyla, and Honor were the ones who needed to be there. I guarantee you, no one missed me."

"Of course, you were missed," Rhylan says, joining us. Even without seeing him, the dragon's deep voice is hard to mistake. "But we were attacked and there were casualties. The citizens understood. It was important you escorted Shadow home. It's good to see you awake, my friend. There have been a lot of worried visitors over the past two days."

When Doc finishes with the bandages, he steps back. "There, how do you feel?"

I raise my hands to my head and shield my eyes. "Well enough, I suppose. Go ahead and turn on the lights and we'll see how badly my head hurts then."

The silence that follows makes the hair on my arms stand on end. "What is it? What's wrong?"

"I don't want you to panic, my man," Doc says, gripping my arm, "but the lights *are* on. Are you saying you can't see anything?"

I blink, swinging my sightless gaze around me as my heart

begins to race once more. "No. Nothing. My world is in darkness. What does that mean? Am I blind?"

Doc squeezes harder and I'm thankful for the anchor. "I'm not sure what the issue is. Let's not panic until I run a few scans. Maybe there's pressure on your optic nerves or something I missed. Let's take a step back and we'll figure it out."

I focus on his advice not to panic but unfortunately, it's not working. I am panicked... very, very panicked. The buzz in my head gains strength and I curse.

"I am blind."

Author Notes

Written on 08/04/2021

Thank you for reading Honor Restored and continuing with the Guardians of the Fae Realms' harems.

If you enjoyed their story, continue with the second book in Honor's harem—Honor Guards. I'm excited to continue with Lukas, Dune, Tundra, and poor Shadow.

I don't plot my stories much ahead of time because I let the scenes unfold and the characters tell me what happens. I feel bad about Shadow's current state but have no doubt things will turn around for him.

After all, the beauty of romance novels is that you're guaranteed a Happily Ever After.

Don't miss out on what happens next with Honor as she finds her footing with her mates and begins to restore the Amberloq forces.

I promise, it will be a fun and sexy ride.

Grab Honor Guards here.

As always, if you want to check in with me, I welcome the chance to chat. I'm active on FB and pretty good at getting to my emails.

Hugs to all,

JL

Find Me

My Direct Sales Site: Shopify

My books

Web page – www.jlmadore.com

Email – jlmadorewrites@gmail.com

Newsletter – JL Series Updates

One who possesses me. Two who revere me. And one who needs me more than ever.

My mind is spinning. There's so much I want to try, to feel, to do. I want to stay in bed forever...

Except, as the Guardian of the Crown, I have a quadrant to secure and a rebellion to stop. The illegal importing of weapons from the Human Realm has empowered the goblins, making them even more dangerous.

With the Amberloq forces in shambles and my training woefully incomplete, my mates to help me ready for the battles ahead. Sure, they are strong, sexy, and strategic but when the battle line is drawn—*I am the Guardian of the Crown.*

Claim your copy now: Honor Guards

ALSO BY JL MADORE

Book 1 – Captured by the Magi

Book 2 – Jesse and the Magi Vault

Book 3 – The Makings of a Magi Knight

Book 4 – Clash with the Magi Council

Book 5 – The Unstoppable Storme

Club Sanguine

Book 1 – Moonstone Maelstrom

Book 2 - Sunstone Sacrifice

JL's More Traditional M/F, M/M, or Menage

The Watchers of the Gray Series (Paranormal)

Book 1 – Watcher Untethered – Zander

Book 2 – Watcher Redeemed – Kyrian

Book 3 – Watcher Reborn – Danel

Book 4 – Watcher Divided – Phoenix

Book 5 – Watcher United – Seth

Book 6 – Watcher Compelled – Bo

Book 7 – Watcher Unfeigned – Brennus

Book 8 – Watcher Exposed – Taharqa

The Scourge Survivor Series (Fantasy)

Book 1 – Blaze Ignites

Book 2 – Ursa Unearthed

Book 3 – Torrent of Tears

Book 4 – Blind Spirit

Book 5 – Fate's Journey

Book 6 – Savage Love – epilogue novella

Aliens of Atlantis Series (Sci-Fi)

Book 1 – Taryn's Tiderider

Book 2 – Kai's Captive

Book 3 – Alyandra's Shadow